A BROOKHAVEN PARANORMAL COZY MYSTERY
BOOK 2

HIGH TIDE

S.E. BIGLOW

1

It felt strange to say that I'd grown used to the relative silence of Tia Tania's Bed and Breakfast in the few short weeks I'd lived there when I'd been the only other guest. Of course, Vera had lived there for the short time she'd been in Brookhaven before her murder, but it still felt unnatural to have another boarder just two doors down the corridor from me. One would think the unassuming man who'd taken up residence in Room 6 would have been easy to overlook. Yet, I was acutely aware of his presence. Maybe it's because he served as a stark reminder of the unfinished business in this house.

Walter Lawson, our newest boarder, had come to

Brookhaven looking for his missing sister, McKenzie. He was convinced she had come to town and was still here, even though the police had found her ID and phone among Vera's belongings. Plus, the town's Chief of Police, Rick Hayes, had determined that the woman who Walter believed to be his sister, was in fact Vera Chase, girlfriend to a dangerous New York drug dealer. That drug dealer had hunted Vera down, killed her for stealing from him, and tried to frame me in the process.

That mystery still hung like a thick cloud around the bed and breakfast, even as the summer sun shone through the windows in the kitchen in early September. I stood there, coffee mug in one hand, studying the way the plant in the hanger by the window reached toward the sunlight, as if it had never felt the warmth from above before. In the back of my mind, I heard it whispering of its hunger. Since I'd come to stay, Tania had been placing potted plants all over the house. She claimed it was to help keep the air clean. I suspected she had ulterior motives.

It was nearly impossible for me not to hear the call from the greenery around the house thanks to my hedge magic. I was still very much a novice at my craft and I had a hunch this was Tania's not-so-subtle way of forcing me to practice using my skills on something other than marijuana seedlings.

"All right." I sighed as I watched the plant struggling to open its leaves. Setting my mug on the table I moved to stand by the planter and gently pinched the stem below the leaf that remained curled up.

I focused on envisioning what the plant could be if it were only able to open up and soak up the much needed sunlight. The tips of my fingers grew warm where they made contact with the stem and I heard the soft crinkle of a leaf unfurling. When I opened my eyes, the pigment in the leaf had brightened and its whispers of hunger had faded.

"You should feel good about that," Tania's voice said from the other end of the kitchen.

I turned to see my landlady standing there in a sleeveless blouse the color of red wine and a floor length skirt in a complimentary dark purple hue. Even just a few short weeks ago, her statement would have both baffled and discomforted me. Tania is an empath and not shy about reading people, especially in the confines of her home.

"It barely needed my help," I noted and reclaimed my coffee.

"Don't sell yourself short, Darcy. You've been practicing and it shows," she said with a smile.

"Someone hasn't given me much choice," I noted, gesturing into the dining room where she'd placed a window box full of newly sprouted daisies.

She chuckled. "I have gone a little overboard, I suppose."

"I tried to tell her that, but no one ever listens to me," Sam—the bed and breakfast's resident ghost—bemoaned as he materialized wearing a pair of skin-tight leather pants and a sparkly sequin jacket.

"My hero," I teased. I still knew very little about Sam. He was the only ghost I'd ever met. His clothes oscillated between flamboyant and verging on a 70s era Elton John impersonator. I'd made several mental notes to ask Sam about his existence and extensive wardrobe, but had never found the right time to broach the subject.

"Am I interrupting something?" Walter's voice cut into the conversation before Sam could throw a snarky retort back at me.

Despite the fact that Walter had some form of magic, he still couldn't see Sam. Maybe because Sam hadn't warmed to him yet or perhaps because he hadn't used his magic much since arriving in town.

Besides, it wasn't like he had to hide his abilities. As Tania had told me when I'd first settled in Brookhaven a month ago, this town was a safe place for those with magic and other supernatural gifts.

"Nothing important," I said, waving Sam away as I downed the rest of my coffee and set the mug in the sink to soak. "I was just getting ready to head to work."

"I'll walk with you," he offered and pivoted on his heel to open the front door.

I followed him into the oppressive summer heat. As I glanced back over my shoulder at Tania who moved to stand in front of the stove, I hoped she wasn't planning a trek outside in those dark colors. The humidity this early in the morning had already triggered a thin layer of sweat on my exposed fore-arms. Summer in New England was still a new phenomenon for this born-and-bred Brit.

We left the bed and breakfast behind and started down Main Street toward Birch Street, the illumi-nated sign for High Time rising up above us. You couldn't miss it, lit up with a giant shoe sporting a marijuana leaf at its center. Almost on accident I'd landed a job there. My burgeoning plant magic coupled with the fact I'd saved the owner on an insurance claim by uncovering a theft by an employee had put me in the good graces of my boss.

As we walked, I noted the slight slump in Walter's posture. I didn't need to be an empath to sense his anxiety. He'd been trying to track down his sister, McKenzie, because he felt he'd pushed her into exploring her magic before she was ready. Every day that passed without a hint of where she might be hiding wore on his nerves.

"We're going to figure out what happened," I told him as we waited for the walk signal at the light across from High Time. As I waited for him to speak, the ghost of a memory flashed before me. I was in Tania's little VW Bug and we were on our way to the boardwalk for fireworks when a stolen truck had hit us in its getaway. Most people would have never come back after an experience like that, and yet here I was grateful to be in a place that wouldn't make me stifle my powers.

"I just don't understand how she could know I'm here and not at least try to reach out. I'm worried something else might have happened," Walter lamented as the walk sign on the opposite side of the street changed to a pale figure.

"How can you be sure she knows you're here?" I pressed as we crossed to in front of High Time.

I didn't fully comprehend Walter's magic. I knew generally that magic fell into one of two categories: elemental and emotional. It seemed far more common that magic fell on the emotional side of things, like with Tania's empathic abilities. Not to mention Ginny Hayes—town gossip and owner of the only coffee shop in town—who could sniff out the truth. And then there was Maggie, the town's resident healer. I couldn't stop myself from smiling as an image of her with her short hair, strong arms, and kind smile filled my mind's eye. She was beautiful in every way and had saved my hide more than once with her healing magic. But like me, McKenzie's magic according to Walter was elemental. She was drawn to water.

"I know McKenzie's and my abilities are different, but I can just tell that she knows I'm here. But I can't feel if she's scared or angry or misses me." He rubbed at his neck. "I also know that my ability to sense her has diminished in the last few days. I don't know what that means, but it can't be good. If she's left again, I've got no idea where she'd go next."

I was about to suggest we needed Tania's assistance, but it wasn't' my place to rope my landlady into this search. I'd done that enough to her in the last few months. "Have you talked to Chief Hayes about helping you look for her?"

"He's put out some alerts, but says there's not much else he can do. After all it's not like she's done anything to run afoul of the law."

It sounded like an excuse not to do his job, but I have a strained relationship with the local lawman. I'd ended wrapped up in two different investigations in the span of a few months. In fact, I'd even been a suspect one of those times. He was also the person I liked least knowing about my magic. I couldn't quite explain why, but Chief Hayes just rubbed me the wrong way.

"Yeah, but you reported her missing. They should be out searching."

"But I didn't report her missing here. Seems like it's not high profile enough, now that Vera's case has been wrapped up."

Even though until a few weeks ago, McKenzie could have been laying in the morgue.

"Well, like I said, we're going to find her." I should have asked Sam to check his usual haunts to see if she showed up anywhere. After all, she had to eat and sleep. But there'd been no word about any break-ins, stolen food, or clothing. I'd been making it a point to visit Ginny's cafe more frequently just to see if I could catch any snatches of gossip she blared out to the surrounding patrons.

"I'm going to head to the pier. Sometimes I still feel her there. Maybe it's all in my head or some stupid confirmation bias, but it's all I have," Walter said, sounding resigned.

I gave him a small encouraging wave before I headed to the side entrance of High Time. It was still early enough that I didn't expect to see many of my co-workers. I spotted Sage's truck in the parking lot. I might also run into Thomas, one of the bakers. It depended on whether he was on good terms with his roommate. I wanted to tell him he should find a new roommate, but it wasn't my place. We were work friends—the kind of people who shared surface level things once in a while. Not the kind of people who gave life advice, especially unsolicited.

The kitchen was eerily dim and quiet as I walked in. Making the familiar trek through the employee break area and stopping just long enough to pull on my ID badge before heading for the growth room. It was a little more humid than it had been the day before. I closed my eyes, listening to the plants and I could hear their discomfort. Seedlings are very temperamental things. I fiddled with the thermostat on the wall until I heard the ventilation system kick in and begin circulating cooler air.

"That should be better," I said to no one in particular.

"Morning, Darcy," Sage called from the doorway leading out front to the counter where customers made their purchases.

Sage had startling pale blue eyes that matched her turquoise-dyed hair. She wasn't what I'd call a hippie. Though she had far more chill than any person had any right to have, given the tragedies that kept befalling her and her business. She hadn't ever asked me directly if I had magic and I'd never broached the topic myself, but it felt less embarrassing now with her walking in on me conversing with the plants. I could always use the excuse that there was some research that pointed to improved plant growth when you talked to them.

"Morning," I greeted.

"Before things get into full swing, I'm asking everyone to meet in the break room. I made the announcement last night after you left about making sure everyone, even those not on shift this morning came in. Sorry, I meant to tell you sooner."

"Is everything okay?" My heart started hammering in my chest.

"Everything's fine. I'll see you in about ten minutes," she said, patting my arm before moving through the growth room and disappearing from view.

Right when I could have used the distraction of trying to decipher the plants around me, they went quiet. I tried not to let the myriad of possibilities spiral out in my head as I waited, only to hear other voices coming from the kitchen area. I spotted Thomas' head bob in and out of view, and took that as my cue to go join everyone else.

There wasn't more than about twenty people all told, but we also didn't generally all come in at the same time or occupy the same space. So, the break room felt cramped as I squeezed in beside Thomas. He offered me a friendly smile and tucked a dread-lock up into the hairnet around his head.

"Thanks everyone for coming in. I know for some of you this your day off," Sage began and a hush fell over the room. "Now, I know it feels a bit ominous when the boss calls a big meeting with everyone for practically the crack of dawn—"

"You aren't shutting down are you?" Sherry, one of the confectioners interrupted.

"No, the business is fine. In fact, we're up over last quarter," Sage replied. "I wanted to acknowledge that we've been through a bit of a rough patch the last few months and I really appreciate that all of you have stuck with me. It was your support that kept my spirits high."

Someone on the far side of the room started a slow clap that got half a dozen more people in on it before it died down. Sage chuckled and waved off whoever had started it.

"So, to say thank you, I wanted to announce that we will be closed for Labor Day weekend and I've bought everyone tickets for the harbor cruise on Monday. Now, it is not mandatory," she paused and looked at one of the other hair netted employees on the opposite side of the room, "I know some of you aren't fond of boats. But I wanted to make the offer and for those of you who aren't interested in the cruise, I'm offering a voucher for the price of the tickets as an extra bonus on top of your holiday pay. I hope you'll at least come out to the pier with the rest of us."

A mixture of excitement and apathy went up from my co-workers. I'd seen the harbor cruises come through when I'd been down on the pier. I'd been under the impression they were shutting down for the summer. Maybe this was one last hurrah before the boats were moored for fall and winter?

Either way, it appeared to be a fun way to spend a free weekend. Anyways, being close to the water, maybe I'd get lucky and find a clue that might lead me to McKenzie and give Walter some much-needed good news.

2

$\mathcal{I}$ didn't think through the fact that Sage's team-building activity involved actually being out on the water. I've never been a huge fan of open water. When I was about seven, I'd gone on a trip with my parents and they'd insisted we do some whale watching. The sea had been rough and the weather had turned from sunshine into strong gusts and downpouring rain as soon as we left the dock behind. The captain had been a stubborn old bloke, who insisted that we'd paid for the time. I'd been miserable and spent the entirety of the trip below deck trying not to lose my breakfast.

"Sage did say she didn't mind people staying on land," Tania reminded me on Monday morning as I gripped a mug of chamomile tea to calm my nerves.

"I feel like I'm still so new that I ought to go just to get to know people," I replied.

"That is very brave of you," Tania said.

"Well, try not to ruin that outfit," Sam chittered from his ghostly perch across the table from me.

"Worrying about her clothes isn't going to help," Tania chided in a disapproving tone.

"What? I'm dead, not blind. That outfit is gorgeous. It would be a tragedy to ruin it," he argued.

"I'll do my best," I offered as my stomach did a flip.

"You could also just take sea sickness medication," Tania pointed out.

Maybe a stop by the pharmacy wasn't a bad idea. I felt a blush creep up the nape of my neck at the thought of seeing Maggie again. *She's not the only person who works there*, I reminded myself as I rinsed the mug and set it to dry before grabbing my purse.

"Where are you headed?" Walter called from the second to last step of the stairs leading to the second floor.

"Pharmacy for some sea sickness medication. Sage is taking us on a cruise off the pier and I'm afraid I've got a weak stomach," I admitted.

"I didn't realize they were still running," Walter said. "Why didn't I think of that?"

"Sorry?"

Walter shook his head. "Every time I've gone down there looking for McKenzie, I've been on land. I'm starting to think that's part of why I can't find her," he answered.

"You think being on the water might help you pick up on her signal?"

"It might. Or give me some hint as to where she might be." Walter pivoted on his heel, racing back up the stairs.

I left him to whatever plan he was hatching and went in search of Maggie. I'd made it half a block before I realized she probably wasn't working, given today was a holiday. I made a show of checking the clinic anyway. Noting the darkened interior and walked the brief trek to Maggie's apartment. I rang the buzzer to the top floor unit and waited.

"Hello?" Maggie's voice came through the speaker.

"Maggie, it's Darcy. Sorry to bother you on your day off, but I was hoping I could beg a favor," I said wringing my hands.

The door buzzed open in response and I climbed the stairs to the third floor. She already stood in the doorway when I reached the landing. She wore denim shorts and a tank top that showed off her broad, muscular build.

"What can I do for you?" she asked.

My mouth went dry as I reached her. It seemed silly now, coming all this way when I probably could have gotten medication from Tania. In that moment, I could hear Maggie scoffing at my request and calling it the pretense it clearly was.

"I ... uh, I'm going on a river cruise with Sage and some other people from work and open water doesn't really agree with me. I didn't know if you had something that might help?" It came out in a single rushed breath of air.

"You do know they sell Dramamine at the store, right?" she said with a soft laugh before ushering me in.

"I remembered that right before I got here. I can just go to the store ..." I said, hooking a thumb over my shoulder toward the stairs when she cut me off.

"Don't be silly. Come on in. I'll mix something up for you."

It felt comfortable being in her living room-kitchen combo. I watched as Maggie disappeared into the bathroom, returning with a jumble of containers in her hands. She spread them on the kitchen counter and began mixing their contents together in a small glass jar. I tried to peer over her shoulder to get a better look, but it was as if she sensed me and angled her body to block my view. After a few minutes, she turned on the tap and filled the jar with water. I caught the sound of a metal cap screwing on and she shook the liquified concoction with a sloshing sound before pivoting and offering it to me.

"How much do I owe you?" I asked, taking the jar of murky bluish purple liquid.

"A review of how well it works." She must have noted the confusion on my face, because she added, "I've never technically made anything for sea sickness before. So, you're kind of my guinea pig. If it works for you, let me know, and maybe I could start offering it at the clinic."

If anyone other than Maggie had admitted to making me their guinea pig, I would have been offended. Coming from her, it was almost sweet. "I think I can manage that. So, should I just drink it all now?"

"I'd start with a few sips right before you get on the water and see how it works. Then take more as needed."

I tucked the jar under my arm and stood there awkwardly staring at her. "Right. Thanks."

"I hope you're able to have fun. What cruise are you doing?"

"Uh, you know, I didn't realize there was more than one to be honest and Sage didn't mention it."

I'd seen boats coming and going the last few weeks, but hadn't paid much mind to whether they were different companies or not. Maybe it was ignorant of me to assume that one boat tour was the same as another?

"There's quite a few that come through here, usually from down the Cape. Like I said, have fun."

That signaled the end of our conversation and I said goodbye as my phone buzzed in my pocket, letting me know I was going to be late if I didn't haul it to the pier. I patted the jar one last time before retracing my steps to the street. I moved with deliberate steps toward the boardwalk. I paused long enough to check my phone and the group text Sage had sent last night on where to meet up to get our tickets.

I spotted Sage standing at the outer edge of a cluster of other familiar faces and I hurried on. Her brightly colored hair was a good beacon to draw the eye, but the sign Thomas held above his head with

High Time's logo provided an extra level of confirmation.

"Hey, Darcy. Glad you made it," Sage said when she spotted me.

"Hope I haven't missed the good stuff," I answered.

She shook her head, aqua-colored hair bobbing around her cheeks. She passed me a paper ticket. "No. The boat's just pulling into dock now. We'll board in a few minutes and be back here this evening."

I shifted the jar of Maggie's sea-sickness concoction, wishing that my magic allowed me to shrink things. Thomas stepped closer, the ends of his dreadlocks fluttering in the breeze.

"You know this is still a work thing, right?"

"It's for seasickness," I replied.

He winked, as if he didn't believe me before returning to his sign holding duties. I swallowed the nerves clenching my throat tight as I spotted the boat pull into harbor. *Time to get this over with.* I unscrewed the lid, pressed the rim of the jar to my lips and drank. I didn't want to find fault with Maggie on the job she'd done, but the taste could use some refining. I gave an involuntary shudder as the concoction settled in my stomach. Turning my attention to the boat we're meant to board; I studied the exterior of the hull. Anything I could do to distract myself from the fact we would soon be out on open water. The lower half of the hull in the water took on a muted blue-grey tone when the sunlight hit it. The rest of the siding wasn't white; at least it hadn't been white in some time. Eggshell might be a better description with faded purple horizontal lines running under the upper deck, framing the name 'Merchant Day Cruises' in a tilted blocky script. The name was the least faded part of the exterior. I made a mental note to tell Maggie which cruise we'd gone on the next time I saw her.

The vessel itself wasn't large. Not that I had any real grasp of boat measurements, but if it could hold more than fifty people, I'd be surprised. Not knowing the number of passengers already on the boat, I eyed our group warily. A quick tally of the people I recognized clustered around Sage and Thomas only added up to ten. Turning to look back down the boardwalk, I spotted a few others milling about, visiting the shops along the pier. At least we wouldn't have to worry about being over capacity.

I expected to see more people come up on the boat's deck, given the warm weather. Plus, I assumed given Brookhaven's reputation as being supernatural, a boat tour would have brought more interest. Then again, I still had trouble believing most normal people took the truth of the town's inhabitants seriously. I'd been skeptical my first time here, too. But back then, I'd been struggling with how to accept my own supernatural abilities. Though that didn't mean my powers were a known thing by everyone. Sage still thought I just had a green thumb. And the less Ginny Hayes thought about me period, the better. The deck of the boat remained barren as the boat settled against the dock and a motorized gangplank descended, making contact with the wooden pier with a clanging *'thud.'*

"Aren't people going to get off and explore?" I questioned, nudging Sage in the shoulder.

She turned, brushing strands of hair behind her ear. "When we come back this afternoon, there will be time for the folks who paid for the longer cruise to come explore the town."

"So, where are we going, then?" I probed.

Sage didn't have time to answer before a stocky man with a thinning hairline and a bushy beard descended the gangplank. He produced a clipboard and paper ledger. I assumed he was the captain, but he wasn't wearing any of the traditional garb I'd associate with the position. No hat or jacket with shiny brass fasteners and no oversized hat. Just a light windbreaker over his navy blue t-shirt and wrinkled khakis. The rest of the High Time employees who'd decided to go on the excursion queued in front of me. The line affording me just enough time to pop into a nearby shop to buy a small bag to stow the jar in before handing over my ticket and setting foot on the deck.

"Wait, I have a ticket," Walter called, sprinting down the pier toward us.

The man taking tickets scowled, but accepted the ticket and let him on. Walter clung to the railing long enough to catch his breath and give me a small wave. When the last of the new passengers were aboard, the bearded man disappeared around a structure I had to assume housed the engine and navigation controls. I gripped the railing along the side of the boat next to Walter as I watched the water beneath ebb and flow, bobbing us up and down. The contents of my stomach sloshed and I sucked in a deep breath, holding it. I could handle a little open water. As the boat's engine revved and churned the water into a frothy foam behind us, I watched Walter turn his back to the pier. His gaze was focused out on the expansive body of water before us. I suspected he hoped to find some clue that might point to McKenzie's whereabouts.

"To the ladies and gentlemen who have just joined us, please make your way below deck for some light refreshments. We've had some choppy seas today so being below deck should provide as smooth a ride as possible. We will be at Haven Island in approximately thirty minutes," a deep male voice said in a monotone over a crackling intercom.

I trailed Sage down the four stairs at the stern of the boat. Maybe a dozen other passengers sat grouped in small clusters in seats bolted to the walls below deck. Rows of benches took up the center of the space with a small table along the opposite wall, boasting what looked like a carafe of coffee and some pastries with some sort of nuts crumbled on top of them.

I had no desire to give my stomach more reason to revolt, so I sat in one of the seats nearest the stairs and watched my co-workers settle in on the benches around me. A few of them meandered through the cramped space to get coffee or food, but most simply found space as the boat's engine continued to thrum, droning in my ears. The inability to hear or hold a conversation below deck outweighed the relative stability the room afforded. Walter was the last to join us and crammed himself into a seat closest to the front of the boat, beside a small circular window. I turned my attention to the other passengers seated along the opposite wall.

I had no way of knowing if they were one large group or several smaller ones, but the way they sat sequestered from each other suggested at least two groups. One was a family with two squirming children who kept pivoting in their seats, staring out the windows, jabbing their stubby fingers against the glass as they spotted whatever amused them. The woman who accompanied them kept reaching over and trying to force them to sit facing inwards without much luck.

The second group consisted of all adults who looked bored by the whole experience. Two men sat buried nose-deep in their phones while two women glanced across the room at the food, maybe deciding on whether to risk it as the boat undulated on the waves.

"Sorry for the rough seas, folks. We should be through the worst of it in a few minutes," the same male voice announced.

Trying to distract myself from the discomfort, I rotated in my seat. Leaning one elbow on the back of the bench, watching the open water rise up around us through the small porthole. I thought I could make out the edges of a small land mass ahead of us, slowly growing larger and more defined as we raced toward it. For a fleeting moment I could swear I saw a dark head of hair appear from beneath a wave close to shore. The figure turned and I could swear she looked eerily similar to Vera Chase.

McKenzie.

"Welcome to Haven Island. We will be docking shortly. Passengers are welcome to get off and explore the area," the male voice said and just as his voice faded over the loudspeaker, so too did the distant figure in the water.

I sucked in a breath as the boat slowed. I could make out a dock through the tiny window and glanced over at Walter who still sat glued to his own window. Had he seen what I had? Or had it just been the water playing with my imagination? I wasn't looking for more mysteries to solve today. I only wanted a nice day off.

3

The family with the small children were first on deck, followed by the two women in the other group. I led the pack for High Time's employees, grateful to see land only a few meters away. I gazed out at the sandy beach that greeted us, backed by a copse of trees. A slender woman in a vibrant purple dress that could have matched the logo on our boat if it hadn't been so weather-beaten approached as people disembarked.

"Good morning everyone. Please gather around," the woman called, waving her hands to urge stragglers off the boat and onto dry land. "My name is Corinne Toomey and I want to welcome you all to Haven Island."

The moment my feet met the sandy ground of

the island, the hairs on the backs of my arms bristled in warning. If Beau had been with me, I could have discreetly asked him what might be sending up danger signals. But my telepathic friend hadn't come on this trip and as magical as he might be, I didn't think he had the ability to teleport or read my thoughts from such a distance.

I tried to ignore the unease as the rest of the High Time contingent and Walter joined the tour group. Corinne flashed a wide, no-doubt practiced smile at everyone. She clapped her hands together to put the focus back on herself. "I will be your liaison while you're on the island today. Just a few ground rules before you get started. First, please be mindful that the island has several private residences. They are, of course, private property and entering them without permission is against the law. So, let's avoid that, okay? And second, some of the plants on the island are ... unfriendly to humans. We've done our best to mark them with orange markers."

"I can't believe I let you talk me into bringing the kids here," the woman who now toted the smaller child in her arms sniped at the man she'd come with.

"Oh, come on, they'll be fine," he responded as

the older child swung his hand back and forth like a pendulum.

"You know Simon runs off the minute you let go of his hand," the woman argued.

"And that's why I brought the backpack," the man answered, producing a small pack with a monkey's tail leading to a wrist strap.

"Excuse me, do you have printed maps or anything?" Sage asked loudly, drowning out the couple's bickering and wrangling of little Simon into the pack.

"I'm afraid not. But the island is equipped with a very good Wi-Fi signal and if you go to Brookhaven's town website you'll find a digital map of the island. Now, if you would follow me."

Corinne spun on her heel and it was then I realized she was wearing actual heels. The move left a neat hole in the sand when she marched toward the tree line with all of us in tow. I should have been using the short trek to more stable footing to take in our surroundings, but I couldn't stop my brain from questioning why anyone would wear such impractical shoes on an island.

"Who thinks to grow poisonous plants on an inhabited island?" one of the men who'd been glued to his phone remarked as we followed Corinne through a clearly marked space amongst the trees and into a more populated area. The sand gave way to paved streets. I spotted rows of tiny orange flags as she led us to a small single-story wooden building with a painted sign hanging over the front door reading 'Ollie's Oddities.' I spotted another wooden structure up the way with smoke billowing from a chimney.

"You are welcome to explore the main part of the island," Corinne said, then consulted her watch. "Please be back here before two o'clock. The boat leaves promptly and I'm afraid your vessel is the only one coming to the island today."

The family, little Simon in the lead with his monkey backpack, took off in one direction, while some of my co-workers, Thomas included, headed for Ollie's Oddities. I stayed rooted to the spot, immobilized by indecision. I'd come here looking to relax and get to know my co-workers. Yet I couldn't stop wondering if Walter was right and this place might hold some clue to finding his sister.

"First time off the main land?" Corinne's voice was jarring in my ear when I realized she'd moved to stand beside me.

"I'm not much for open water," I answered.

She reached a manicured hand over and patted

my shoulder. "You're on dry land now, honey. Have a look around."

"You know, I was curious about the island, if you don't mind answering a few questions," I said, an idea forming in my head.

"Sure."

I played up the foreigner angle to feed into her sense of ego. If she thought she was educating me, she might be more willing to share information she would normally keep to herself. "I'm not from around here. Well, I mean, I live in Brookhaven, but I'm a recent transplant," I began.

"I had a suspicion you weren't local," she said with an exaggerated wink.

"So, you can imagine, I'm still learning loads about this area of the United States. To be honest, until we got on the boat, I didn't know this island even existed."

"Well, the town of Brookhaven purchased the island about eighty years ago from the government. Most of the flora here is native. We brought in some of the trees you see along the beach, but everything else was already growing here."

I gestured to the neon orange markers nearest us. "Couldn't you just get rid of them?" Even as I asked the question, my chest ached at the thought. Before discovering my plant magic, I hadn't been the world's biggest fan of leafy green things. Now I had a healthier respect for them.

"Oh, they tried." She leaned in close and whispered, "Unfortunately it's how we learned so many of them seemed to be poisonous. In the end, developers found it was easier to just mark them off."

"And you mentioned private residences. I assume they're wealthy."

She nodded. "Most come from New York or Boston. Old money, that sort of thing. But every now and then we'll have a tour. Usually at the start of summer."

"So, do you see a lot of people come through this time year? I imagine it's better to visit an island now than when everything's frozen over."

Corinne's bright demeanor slipped and she pulled her hand away from me. She glanced over her shoulder, like she expected someone to eavesdrop on our conversation. I thought I caught Walter out of the corner of my eye making his way back toward the beach. "Business hasn't been as booming as in the past, but I'm sure it will pick up again next season."

"Are the cruises the only way people can get here?"

Her gaze narrowed at me and her lips pinched in at the corners. "We are open to the public through contracts with tour companies. As I thought was obvious, the people who live here value their privacy. We don't just let people onto the island without verifying where they've come from." She cleared her throat. "If you'll excuse me, I have to check in with some folks."

She took off at a sprint and it was a wonder she didn't fall flat on her face. Our question-and-answer session hadn't been nearly as illuminating as I'd hoped. If McKenzie was here, she'd either come by boat like the rest of us or had managed to stay hidden. The first option seemed nearly impossible given that Vera had stolen her ID and wallet whenever they'd crossed paths weeks earlier. You needed money to be able to buy passage on a boat. But I also doubted a random stranger appearing out of the ocean would have gone unnoticed.

Time to have a look around. *Try to relax Darcy*, I told myself. Walter was here, too. He could go searching for McKenzie if he chose. Yes, I'd promised we would find her, but I was meant to be on holiday today. I took a few steps closer to the vegetation marked with the orange flags and closed my eyes. I waited to see if the sense of danger that had washed over me when we'd first arrived was just my magic telling me that there were plants here that wanted to do me and other people harm.

The sense of foreboding danger didn't hit me again, even as I stepped closer and held out a hand. I didn't go so far as to touch the plants. Still, as I concentrated, I conjured the image of my magic in my mind's eye as Maggie had taught me to do. Where once it had taken ages to get the manifestation of my magic to grow from a seedling into a thriving flower, today it was in full bloom and ready to react to the world around me. Opening my eyes, I knelt by the orange marker and inhaled. Nothing in the look or scent of the plant betrayed its deadliness. I could feel the plants around me stirring, awakening to my presence. They didn't feel malevolent to me.

This is a strange place.

Straightening up to my full height, I realized I was alone on the main street. Most of the rest of the passengers had funneled into Ollie's Oddities. Instead, I ventured toward the other building with the smoke still billowing from the chimney.

The sign on the front door appeared hand painted and lettered, announcing the dwelling as simply 'The Tea Shoppe.' The door sat ajar and I could hear a hoarse voice coming from within. I pulled the door fully open to reveal a cramped space with shelves lining the walls from floor to ceiling. I could see tiny colored tins containing what I assumed to be tea, based on the place's name. I spotted one of the women who'd been in the group of four on the boat. Her face shone with a layer of sweat as she leaned against the counter. I didn't see anyone else in the tiny space.

"You were on the Merchant cruise," I said, stepping up beside the woman.

"What?" she croaked.

"The day cruise. You were on the boat, weren't you?" I repeated.

"Oh, yeah," she answered, rubbing at her chest.

I spotted a large stone hearth that took up one full wall behind the counter leading to the chimney with multiple large kettles at various states of boiling. I could feel sweat bead under my arms in a matter of minutes from being inside the shop.

"I know we don't know each other, but you don't look well. Maybe getting out in the air will help? I know this heat's making me a bit woozy," I said and gestured to the door I'd left open.

"Waiting for an order," she managed before she started coughing.

I cast about, trying to find something to help. A bottle of water or something to fan her with, but came up empty. So, I hedged my bets and grabbed her by the forearm.

"Come on, you need some air."

She didn't fight me as I led her outside. Being out of the smoke and steam seemed to ease her breathing enough for her coughing fit to stop.

"There, that's better. Can I maybe find you some water?" I offered. The only liquid I had on me was Maggie's sea sickness concoction and I doubted it would help this woman.

"That ... that would be good," she answered.

"Stay here, I'll be right back."

I left the woman—whose name I ought to have gotten before leaving her unattended—behind and made a beeline for Ollie's Oddities. The door sat partially open and I could feel a cold blast of air conditioning hit me in the face when I crossed the threshold. Where the Tea Shoppe had been overwhelmingly cramped, Ollie's shop was spread out and neatly organized. There was a tasteful display of small trinkets that bore a placard touting that they were handmade. A small bin of prepackaged snacks, including almonds, lined the wall behind the counter. There were a few novelty hats and shirts hung along the far wall and a portly balding man sat behind the counter, hands clasped in front of him.

"Hi there, welcome to Ollie's. I'm Ollie," he greeted.

"Hi, do you sell water by chance?"

He nodded, gesturing to a small cooler tucked under one of the shelves on the far wall. I crossed the tight space and pulled out a bottle before returning to the counter and placing it on the counter between us.

"Let me guess, you were in Paula's shop weren't you?" he said and rang up my purchase.

"How'd you guess?"

He chuckled. "I've never met a woman who liked heat more than her, but it's a bit much for most customers. They'll go and get their fancy teas and then come right over here to cool down. It's why I've got the air blasting so high."

"Well, thanks for this," I said and left the chilly atmosphere behind.

I retraced my steps to the Tea Shoppe, but the woman was gone. I checked the shop and found it empty. The kettles had stopped boiling, so maybe Paula had come back to tend to them. I did a quick sweep up the street, but quickly found high metal gates bearing signs to keep off the private property.

The only logical direction she could have gone was back toward the beach. I hadn't seen her pass by Ollie's store and I'd only been in there a minute or two at most.

The tingling on the back of my arms returned and I hurried along the street, reaching the tree line just as I heard raised voices coming from ahead of me. I picked up my pace and broke through the foliage to find the woman I'd met at the tea shop lying in the sand. The rest of the passengers from our cruise, minus Walter, stood huddled not far from her. The couple were shielding their children's view.

"What happened?" I called to the others.

No one answered. They just looked around, helpless. For most of the people standing on the beach, this was the first emergency like this they'd encountered. Oh, how I wished I was as ignorant as them.

I staggered to a halt by the woman to find her eyes wide, her face wet not with sweat, but sea water. I could smell the brine on her skin and see water in her partially open mouth. I couldn't begin to explain how that could be possible when the rest of her clothes were dry and she was a good three feet from the waterline. The saltiness around her triggered my gag reflex and I sucked in a deep breath to keep from vomiting. The water bottle fell from my fingers as I reached down and pressed two fingers to the pulse point on her neck.

Please be alive.

Nothing.

I didn't believe in curses—although given the existence of magic, maybe I should start—but I was beginning to feel like someone had put one on me. This woman had been alive, if a bit overheated, the last time I'd seen her. Only now, here she lay dead. How did I keep ending up in these situations?

4

"Oh God, what happened?" Corinne's voice spurred me to action.

I stood, feet sinking in the sand around the dead woman's body as I looked at our island liaison. "She's dead. You need to call the police."

Corinne's body trembled as she took in the sight of the body and I freed myself from the sand to reach her. I gripped her wrists to keep her as calm and steady as I could manage. "Please, call the police. You said Brookhaven owns this land. That means their police have jurisdiction here, too, right?"

"Y-yes."

"Good. Call them," I repeated.

Slowly, the trembling stopped and she produced a cell phone—from where I didn't want to know—and I watched her dial 9-1-1. For a moment I was grateful that the police would soon be on scene. They could find out what had happened to this poor woman. Then I remembered that Brookhaven only had two police officers and one of them was not my biggest fan. I could almost hear Chief Hayes demanding to know why I was wrapped up in yet another mess in his town.

I left her to convey our location to the authorities and went to join my co-workers who stood huddled in a tight knot away from the body. "What happened?"

"We were thinking of going swimming," Monica, one of the bakery assistants said in a strained tone.

"Did you lot find her, then?" I probed, realizing too late that my tone came across as accusatory.

"We didn't notice her at first," Thomas said, his voice clearer than Monica. "We were down at the other end of the beach when we heard a scream. I think one of the people she was with found her. Or maybe it was the lady with the kids."

I glanced about, but saw no sign of the woman's three companions. That seemed strange. Still I had nothing but a gut feeling to base it on. It also worried me that I hadn't seen Walter in some time. I had no doubt he was off looking for McKenzie, but had he seen something, too? I filed it away for later assessment and tried to build whatever timeline I could.

You aren't investigating anything. Stop it.

"I saw her at the tea shop not five minutes before. I'd gone to get her some water. I must have been too distracted to realize she'd gone by," I sighed.

"It looked like she just collapsed," Sage offered somberly.

"She'd been sweating, a lot," I noted. But even though the summer heat was oppressive to my British sensibilities, I doubted it was enough to cause her to die from heat stroke. Besides, it wouldn't explain the smell of sea water on her body.

"Excuse me," Corinne's voice cut through our conversation. "The police will be here in fifteen minutes. They want everyone off the beach."

"Where are we supposed to go?" Simon's mother demanded, rocking her younger child in her arms.

"We have a staff compound where you can wait."

I started toward the path through the trees, assuming the staff compound was hidden away somewhere off the main street. Corinne hurried to get in front and the rest of the High Time contingent fell in behind me. I could hear the woman trying to calm her child while Simon's father argued with him about following directions.

We marched past Ollie's Oddities and I could see Ollie peer out his open doorway with interest. But not enough to leave the safety of his air conditioning to find out what was going on. The Tea Shoppe's door was now closed. Corinne led us down a side street—I hadn't noticed in my brief exploration of the main thoroughfare—to a squat concrete structure. She keyed in a code and the door released with a pneumatic hiss and loud 'beep.' It reminded me of the bomb shelters littered throughout London from World War II.

What kind of island needs a bomb shelter? Maybe it's for hurricanes?

Bright LED lights came on the moment Corinne stepped into the space, illuminating a few desks, a water cooler, and a coffee maker. Once the group who'd been on the beach crammed into the space, Corinne cleared her throat.

"Let me see if I can find some chairs. Please stay here."

"Not like we've got anywhere else to go," Simon's father griped, to which the boy's mother let out an irritated huff.

"You ever get the feeling there's some cruel master of fate out there who gets off on putting you in horrible situations?" Sage asked, stepping up beside me.

If I hadn't known better, I'd have sworn she was a telepath. But I had spent enough time around her and around people with magic to tell the difference. "I don't want to sound conceited, but I feel like it's me."

"I don't think it's you," Sage countered.

"A theft, a dead employee, and now another dead body while on a company excursion. And things only started happening when I came around," I reminded her.

"Correlation is not causation," she retorted. "You had nothing to do with the theft or Vera's death, well except for helping find out the truth. And I'm pretty sure you didn't kill that woman."

Had my magical senses been warning me about the impending death? I wasn't foolish enough to think it wasn't foul play somehow. The salt water and the fact her clothes were dry were just too strange to be a coincidence. Though I had no reason to go nosing about and shouldn't get involved.

"I want to see the mermaid," Simon bellowed,

shedding his monkey backpack, and making a break for the door.

"There are no mermaids," his father called.

Given the presence of witches and ghosts in Brookhaven, I wouldn't bet against mermaids being real. Though I suspected Simon had seen something or rather someone else. Maybe Walter's hunch about coming out here to look for McKenzie hadn't been wishful thinking on his part after all.

I moved to put myself in the boy's path and bent down to his level. He skittered to a halt in front of me. "You saw a mermaid?"

He nodded. "On the beach."

"I didn't know mermaids could go on the beach," I said nonjudgmentally.

"She had legs. Like in the movie."

"What did the mermaid do?"

"I don't know. But she went away. I want to see her again."

Some people might not put stock in a child's experience, but he was innocent and had no reason to lie. He'd seen someone come out of the water and disappear back in again. It had to be McKenzie.

This only raised more questions. Why would McKenzie want a perfect stranger dead? It might explain the water on the woman's face, though. Simon's father reached a hand out and yanked the boy back, fixing me with an exasperated glare. I guess he didn't appreciate how I'd indulged his little boy's fantasy.

The door to the structure beeped again and hissed open, revealing Corinne with the dead woman's original group from our cruise, and Walter, plus the man who'd taken our tickets and who I now realized was our captain. Two familiar faces trailed behind them. Vinnie spotted me first and offered a sad smile with a discreet wave. I didn't return the gesture. I didn't need to attract any more attention than I'd already received from him. We were in a crowded room with twenty people, the more anonymous I could be, the less chance I'd wind up in the Chief's crosshairs.

Somehow, the moment Chief Hayes looked up from the notepad in his hand, our gazes met and I did my best not to squirm. His brown eyes always carried an intensity accented by flashes of amber in his irises.

"Ladies and gentlemen, I'm sorry to have to interrupt your visit, but we're going to need to get statements from everyone," Chief Hayes began before turning to Vinnie. "Please ensure the scene is secure and wait for the coroner. They should be arriving within the hour."

"Yes, sir."

Vinnie spun on his heel and left the group alone with the Chief of Police. Given the influx of crime befalling the town, I was surprised he hadn't tried to hire more officers. Then again, the temporary help he'd hired during Vera's case had missed my little breaking and entering. Not that I was proud of sneaking into the police station and borrowing evidence to try and track down my former co-worker's killer.

"I'm going to need somewhere private to conduct my interviews," Chief Hayes told Corinne.

She gestured to a door at the back of the compound. "You can use the server room. It's the best we have," she answered.

"It will do." The Chief's gaze moved from person to person, landing on me. "I'll take Ms. Ingram's statement first."

Swallowing my nerves, I followed him and Corinne to the room marked 'Private.' Corinne entered a code into another electronic keypad before pushing the door inward, revealing rows of sleek servers and an industrial cooling unit. The people who lived on this island really must have been made of money to have such sophisticated equipment.

"Please wait outside," he instructed Corinne.

She eased the door shut and I stood there amidst the humming and whirring technology, trying not to let Brookhaven's Chief of Police's imposing presence unnerve me. He flipped open his notepad and gestured for me to take a seat in the single metal chair pushed against one wall.

"I'd like to say I'm surprised to see you at the scene of a dead body, Miss Ingram, but unfortunately we both know that isn't the case."

"I'd tell you I had nothing to do with it, but we both know it isn't in your nature to take what I say at face value," I retorted.

"Why don't we start with what you were doing on Haven Island today?"

"I was here with Sage and some other employees from High Time. We were supposed to be doing a bit of bonding."

"And you arrived here via Merchant Day Cruises?"

"That's right. Sage booked the tickets. I've got the paper one she gave me if you need to see it."

He waved off my offer. "What can you tell me about the woman on the beach?"

"I met her on the boat. Well met is a strong word. I saw her on the boat. I never even got her name. We ran into each other in the Tea Shoppe. She wasn't looking well and I offered to get her some water."

"And where did you get the water?"

"Ollie's Oddities. It was just up the street. I was there maybe five minutes. I left her at the tea shop, but when I went back she was gone."

"You didn't see her leave?"

"I was a bit preoccupied with trying to get her water. I went looking for her. I checked the area that led to the private residences, but there was no sign of her. So, I headed back to the beach, because I figured that's the only other place she might go."

"Then what happened?"

"I heard yelling and when I got to the beach I saw her lying there in the sand. She wasn't moving and no one else was near her."

"So, it was the two of you alone on the beach?"

"No. The rest of the High Time staff and the family with the two little ones were there, but no one was close. I checked for a pulse, but she was dead."

"And did you move or otherwise tamper with the body?"

"Of course not! I checked to see if she was alive

and that was all. But I thought something seemed off."

"Off how?" he probed, his hand scribbling notes furiously on his pad.

"When I'd seen her in the tea shop, she was sweating. It was extremely hot in there. Her face was wet when I found her, but it wasn't sweat. At least not all of it. I could smell sea water on her face."

"You're suggesting she might have what ... tried to drink ocean water?"

I stopped short of telling him about Simon seeing who I assumed was McKenzie on the beach. He might believe me about my magic. He'd seen it for himself in the past, but that didn't mean he'd believe me if I told him there was a woman out there who might be living in the ocean. Besides, he hadn't exactly been keen to make her missing person's case a priority.

"I don't know. But her clothes were dry and I thought that was strange. I thought it was important to tell you. That's all I know."

"Thank you." He gestured to the door. "That's all for now. Once I've finished interviewing the rest of the witnesses, we'll arrange for Vinnie to bring everyone back to Brookhaven."

As interactions with Rick Hayes went, this hadn't

been anywhere near the top of the most uncomfortable ones. Maybe we were far enough out of his usual jurisdiction he assumed I couldn't muck things up.

"Oh, the woman who died, I think she was part of a group with the three people you came in with. They weren't on the beach when I found her. I have no idea where they were."

"Noted." He exhaled slowly through his nose. "For the record, Miss Ingram, I don't think you had anything to do with this."

This time.

Still, he didn't have to say that. I pulled the door to the room open and paused on the threshold. "Who should I send in?"

He rubbed his chin. "Just get Ms. Toomey."

I found Corinne pacing the short distance between the coffee maker and the far wall. The rest of the passengers were clustered tightly together with the people they knew. Walter stood off to one side, alone. He kept glancing toward the only way out of the building. The people who'd come with the dead woman kept eying each other, as if they thought the others might have done something.

"He's asking for you," I told Corinne.

Her head snapped to attention and she smoothed a wrinkle in her dress. "Thank you."

I watched her go and wound my way back to the huddle of High Timers. I perched on the edge of the desk that sat perpendicular to the wall and fished my phone out of the bag I'd bought. I had a missed text from Tania.

How is the trip? Hope all is well.

I suspected Chief Hayes would frown upon me telling my landlady that there'd been another death within the town's jurisdiction. Though he had said he planned to take everyone back to Brookhaven and past experience suggested he would want people to stay around for a day or two while they investigated. They'd need somewhere to stay and I knew a place in need of a little extra money.

It's gotten complicated. Can't say more yet, but we may have some extra guests tonight.

Three dots popped up immediately and I waited for her response.

Please be safe.

I would try, but there was a very real possibility that woman had been killed and the killer was still around. It's entirely possible that McKenzie had been hiding on the island undetected and I doubted she would flee now. As far as she knew no one was looking for her here and I bet she thought she'd gone unnoticed on the beach. However, if I'd noticed the possibility she was here, I had every confidence her brother had, too. And if he was this close to finding her, there was every chance Walter wouldn't leave without her.

5

My phone's display read four seventeen by the time the boat's captain stepped out of the server room. Walter had gone in before him and I hadn't had a chance to talk to him, yet. Vinnie returned as well and I resisted the urge to ask him if he'd noticed the salt water on the woman's face. I wondered if there was any way they could determine if the sand around the body had been disturbed by someone else, someone kneeling perhaps? But I kept quiet. When Chief Hayes finally emerged, he pointed to Vinnie and then toward the exterior door.

"We appreciate your patience. We should be able to arrange transport back to the harbor shortly,"

Chief Hayes announced, his voice swallowed up in a gust of wind.

"Can't he just take us? We paid for him for the day," Simon's father griped.

"Have some sensitivity, a woman died. Getting our money's worth isn't important," his wife snapped.

Before they could descend into further bickering, Chief Hayes fixed them with a stern look. "I don't see why Captain Merchant can't take you back to Brookhaven with a police escort." His gazed moved from the couple to Vinnie. "And I'm going to have to ask everyone to not leave Brookhaven for the foreseeable future."

"You can't keep us here," the woman who'd been in the group with the dead woman protested.

"I'm afraid I can and I am. Until we can determine what happened here, we need you close by in case we have more questions."

I swallowed the offer of Tania's Bed and Breakfast, even though I'd already given my landlady a heads up we might be filling rooms tonight. It would be better if Chief Hayes came to the conclusion on his own. There would be less of a chance of him holding it against me later.

As we waited for him to continue, I scanned the

horizon. I could see dark clouds rolling in, promising a summer storm. I wasn't the only one taking notice of the sudden change of weather. Vinnie hurried to close the distance between himself and the Chief, whispering something in the man's ear. Chief Hayes glanced my direction without saying a word before nodding and offering a dismissive hand wave.

"If everyone can please get back on the boat, we're going to head out. For those of you who aren't local to town, the department will put you up at the local bed and breakfast," Vinnie directed.

My shoulders relaxed a fraction as I followed Vinnie back onto the cruise ship. Despite there being the same number of people on the boat, the area below deck felt claustrophobic. The walls pressed in and there wasn't enough room to breathe comfortably. Where before parties had clustered together out of a sense of unfamiliarity, they now separated out of uncertainty.

I tried to figure out what might have prompted McKenzie to reveal herself long enough to interact with the dead woman, but came up blank. I knew very little about McKenzie other than she was a witch and Walter believed she had elemental powers related to water. That made sense given what I had seen today. But it didn't provide any insight into her state of mind. Thankfully, we would be back in Brookhaven in less than thirty minutes and I would have unfettered access to Walter.

Out of the corner of my eye, I caught Vinnie retreating topside, leaving us temporarily unchaperoned. No one else appeared to notice the lack of police presence. No one spoke either. Even my co-workers who knew one another wouldn't meet the gaze of anyone around them.

Taking slow, methodical breaths, I focused on counting the wood panels on the wall across from me. It was better than letting the choppiness of the sea test the strength of Maggie's potion. At least she'd be happy to know it worked for the most part.

I'd reached panel number twenty-four when I felt a hand press on my left shoulder. I tore my gaze away from the paneling to see Vinnie standing beside me, frown lines creasing the skin around his mouth.

"I'm okay," I said, assuming he'd seen my look of determination.

"I realized that I just offered up your home to perfect strangers," he said softly.

"I'm not the one who would have a problem with it. But I think we both know Tania would be more than happy to help the department," I replied, not betraying I'd already warned her.

I realized he must have gone up on deck to call Tania and brief her on the situation. It wasn't polite to show up on a neighbor's doorstep with a gaggle of strangers without giving them some warning even if it was her business. I wanted to ask Vinnie what he'd found on the woman's body. Reminding myself I shouldn't be digging into this only spurred my curiosity more.

"I keep thinking there was something else I could have done. I never even asked her name," I whispered.

Vinnie's jaw worked, as if chewing on his words and weighing what he could and *should* say. "Her name was Sheila Bartow. She was on the cruise with her husband, sister, and brother-in-law ..."

The way his voice trailed off; I knew there was more he wanted to share. Though he was keeping me at arm's length, as he should during an investigation. Vinnie was more tolerant of other people dipping their toes into the world of crime solving than Chief Hayes, but that didn't mean he was open about sharing information he shouldn't. Even the extra information about the other members of her group explained some of the behavior I'd noticed.

Although, if I had a sister who just died, I might have been more distraught than Sheila's sister had appeared. Then again, perhaps the reality hadn't yet set in for them.

"We'll do everything we can to sort this out fast," he offered after a moment of silence.

The boat hit a swell in the water, lurching us up and forward. I felt the meager contents of my stomach rise and fall with the momentum of the boat, and I tightened my grip on the bench beneath me.

"Sorry about that," the captain's voice came over the loudspeaker. "The weather is getting worse, but we should be back to shore in about ten minutes."

"I'm feeling a tad claustrophobic down here. Is it okay if I go above and get some air?" I addressed Vinnie.

"Yeah, of course. But be careful, with the weather getting worse, you don't want to be out there long."

I left the oppressive atmosphere of the lower deck behind, letting the damp air hit me in the face when I ascended the steps. I clung to the railing as the wind tugged at my shirt and hair. It was enough to wash away the nausea that had been threatening to settle back over me. And being able to see the now-familiar boardwalk of Brookhaven growing larger by the second provided a sense of safety. I was coming *home*.

The boat bumped up against the dock a few minutes later and the captain darted past me to tie off the rope and lower the gangplank. I was the first one off the boat and my equilibrium took a moment to reset itself as I took a step away from the gangplank. When I no longer felt the sway of water, I exhaled in relief.

The rest of the High Time staff filed off the boat first. I caught Sage's instruction not to discuss the situation with other people and to make themselves available to Chief Hayes for further questioning if needed. I spotted a few of the employees who'd stayed behind point and whisper at the sight of Vinnie stepping off the boat.

"Ladies and gentlemen, please follow me," he said, addressing the other passengers.

I let him take the lead down Main Street, past Ginny's and the clinic where I spotted Maggie through the front window, and to Tia Tania's Bed and Breakfast. She already stood out front, strands from her greying bob tucked behind her ears.

"Thank you again Tania for offering your home," Vinnie said and shook her hand.

"You know I am always happy to help in any way

I can," she said before addressing our impromptu guests.

"We have plenty of rooms and I've got a hot meal simmering on the stove."

"We weren't planning for a night away," Simon's mother sighed, shifting the younger child to her other hip.

"I'm happy to run and get you what you need," I offered. I knew I'd seen things like diapers at the clinic and it would give me an excuse to see Maggie.

"T-Thank you." She passed the child off to her husband and fished out some bills from her purse. "Some size two diapers and size three as well."

"Do you need formula or anything like that?"

"No, thank you."

I turned to Vinnie. "I swear, I'll be there and back in no time."

He gave me a weary smile and nod before ushering the woman and her family inside behind Tania. I raced back the way we'd come and found Maggie behind the counter in the pharmacy section of the clinic. She appeared to be doing inventory. I could still remember the fluorescent overhead lighting and utilitarian look of the place the first time I'd walked through those doors. Tania and I had just been the victim of a hit and run and Tania had taken me to see the town's healer. It was the first time I'd seen anyone else use magic overtly. The more I'd gotten to know Maggie, the more this place felt welcoming. It was like I belonged here, because she liked me and she thought I belonged.

Maggie looked up from the ledger in front of her. "You made it back in one piece."

"Potion worked. Needs a bit of finessing on the taste," I answered and passed her the half-empty jar.

"Well, I kind of assumed it would need some tinkering. I'm glad it helped. It is rare I have anyone, but myself to test things on. And it's not exactly easy to practice healing on yourself."

"I'll be your test subject any time," I blurted before I could stop myself.

Maggie grinned. "I'll keep that in mind." A pause and then, "So, which company did you end up going with?"

"Merchant Day Cruises."

"They've been in business for years. They don't run too many trips out this way at this time of year, though."

"Well, they've hit some bad luck." Before she could ask me to elaborate, I added, "Anyway, I could use your help again. I'm looking for diapers."

Her brow furrowed, but she pointed to a shelf

along the far wall. "I'm going to need some context."

I left her wondering as I retrieved a small pack of each size and returned to the register. "Not sure how much I should be telling you, but one of the passengers on the cruise died while we were on Haven Island. Chief Hayes wants everyone to stay overnight at least and there was a family with two little ones who were not expecting to spend the night away from home."

Maggie's face took on an air of concern and without a word she disappeared into the clinic. I waited for her to return and when she did, I couldn't help smiling. She produced two blankets and teddy bears with little yellow bows around their necks. "I keep things like this for kids who have to come in. We don't see many, but I had a feeling they might come in handy."

"Brilliant. I think that will really help," I said, tucking the packages of diapers beneath one arm before trying to scoop up the toys and blankets.

"If Rick is involved, I'm guessing it was sudden."

"It ... it looked like she drowned, but none of her clothes were wet, so nothing adds up."

She eyed me. "You've got a theory?"

"More like pieces of information that don't seem to go together. As we got closer to shore, I thought I saw a woman in the water that looked like McKenzie. Also one of the kids says he saw someone come out of the water near the woman's body. And according to Walter, McKenzie's magic is water-based."

"And you're not sure that Rick is going to be able to sort it out if there is magic involved," she said.

How could he?

"I don't know. I can't think of any reason why McKenzie would want to hurt anyone. But then again, maybe she didn't and I'm just missing pieces of the puzzle. I need to get back and talk to Walter. He knows his sister best." I didn't add that he'd joined the cruise last minute and was conspicuously absent when I'd stumbled on the body. I held up my armload of items. "Thanks again for this. And for the potion."

"Glad to be of service."

By the time I made it back to Tania's, the rest of the boat passengers had disappeared inside along with Vinnie and Tania. Walter sat outside on the front porch. Sam hovered nearby, an exaggerated expression of annoyance on his translucent face.

"Here, let me get the door," Walter offered.

"Thanks." I paused on the threshold. "Shouldn't you be inside with the others?"

"I'm just trying to stay out of the way while Tania gets people settled."

I understood. I guessed Sam was out here sulking. For all his complaining about never having anyone at the B&B, he didn't like strangers in his space. I found Simon and his mother sitting in the living room, huddled on one end of the couch. Her eyes lit up at the sight of me.

"Thought these might come in handy, too," I said, offering the toys and blankets.

"That's so nice of you. Thank you," she said, her voice cracking.

Simon latched onto one of the bears and curled up, resting his head on his mother's lap. I set the diapers beside the couch for her and retreated to the front of the house again. Walter stood where I'd left him. Sam had either grown bored or was irritated I hadn't addressed him, because he'd vanished. I swear he was moodier than a teenager, but that let me broach the topic of McKenzie with Walter in private.

"We need to talk," I said pointedly.

"Why?"

"Because a woman is dead and I'm starting to think your sister was either involved or knows something about what happened."

6

My words hung in the air between us for a solid two minutes before Walter blinked, the gesture exaggerated. Finally, he shook his head.

"No, that can't be right. She was confused about what was happening, but she'd never hurt someone."

I wanted to tell him that we didn't always know the people closest to us. After all, I thought I'd known my own family. Yet my parents had denounced my magic and told me I was mental. I still didn't quite understand how I could have this ability if they both lacked it. Everything I knew about magic suggested it was hereditary. Maybe it had skipped a generation? But that wasn't important right now.

"Desperation makes people do things they wouldn't normally dream of," I noted. "But I don't want to believe she's killed someone either. So, tell me everything you know about how her magic works and what it might have done to her state of mind."

"Her powers are elemental, not unlike yours, except her power is drawn from a connection to water." His expression grew wistful. "I should have realized it would turn out to be something like that because she was always in the water as a kid. She loved swimming and just being near water. It didn't matter if it was a pool or a bathtub or the ocean. But we grew up not really knowing about magic."

"Same with me. I didn't know it existed until it just burst out of me one day. It was bloody terrifying," I shared.

"I was pretty freaked out the first time I could sense someone else, too, but I realized it was meant as a gift to help people. But, Kenz, she just panicked."

"You said you tried to talk about it with her and she ran off?"

He nodded. "We'd been close as kids, but as we

grew up we grew apart. I'd hoped this might bring us closer together again. But I think I pushed her to talk about it, to try and explore what she could do too fast."

Something sour and heavy settled in the pit of my stomach that had nothing to do with my recent trip across open water. "Did you ever actually see her use her magic before she took off?"

"Once or twice. I don't think she realized I was watching. I'd sensed her nerves and wanted to show her I could be there for her, even if our powers were different. I mean, how do you tell someone you understand what they're going through when your magic doesn't have a physical manifestation," Walter rambled.

"What did it look like?" I prompted, trying to get him back on track.

He closed his eyes and I could almost see him rewinding images in his memory, trying to picture what he had witnessed. "It was like the water was a living thing, responding to her commands. I don't think she meant to do it at first, but she was washing dishes. The water just came out of the faucet and sort of pooled in her hand." He smiled. "It looked like it was made of clear Jell-O. Another time it looked like she was directing the water to flow in a different direction."

It certainly sounded like the connection McKenzie had to water was similar to how I experienced my own plant magic. That was a good thing. It meant, if I could just find her and talk to her, maybe I could convince her that she didn't have to be afraid of her power. Or like she had to hide it and lash out to protect herself.

"Thank you for that," I said as Walter opened his eyes.

"You can't really believe she'd kill someone."

"I don't want to believe it, but I can't dismiss what I saw.

"And what did you see?" he pressed; voice tight with concern.

I settled on the top step of the porch and he joined me. "Well, on our way to the island, I could swear I saw a woman in the water ... who looked like McKenzie." I had to stop myself from saying it looked like Vera, because Vera was dead. We'd put that mystery to bed already.

"But the way this woman, Sheila, died, was strange. She was far enough from the water that she couldn't have drowned, but I know there was salt water in her mouth."

"She could have gotten pulled out by the tide and washed back in," he noted.

I shook my head. "No, all of her clothing was dry. And there wouldn't have been time for anything like that to happen. Besides, there were a dozen other people there on the beach when I found her. No one had claimed to go diving in after her." I steadied myself for the last bit of news. "And one of the other people saw a dark-haired woman come out of the water near the victim and then disappear again."

Walter hung his head, resting his palms against his forehead. "She wouldn't kill someone. If she was involved, it had to be an accident."

I wanted to believe that too. I wanted there to be a happy ending for Walter and McKenzie. One where they could go home together and learn to use their magic side by side. I wasn't sure I could stomach an ending where he could only visit her through glass in prison.

"Let's say for argument's sake she killed this woman by accident, why would she be there in the first place? And for that matter, why would she be hiding out on the island? Her ID and everything were stolen when she crossed paths with Vera. But she has to know that you are looking for her. You said as much the other day that you knew she could feel you."

"I don't know," Walter answered.

"I know you were looking for her on the island. And you weren't there with everyone else when the police arrived. Where did you go?"

"You're right, I went looking for McKenzie. I spotted her from the boat too. but by the time I got to the area of beach where I assumed she'd be, it was empty. I wandered around for a little bit, but found nothing so I headed back to the main part of the island. That's when I ran into Chief Hayes. I didn't know that anyone had died until then."

I couldn't pinpoint why, but his explanation felt less than truthful. He had reasons to be tight-lipped though. After all, I'd falsely accused him of murder weeks ago. Even if I'd promised to help find his sister, that betrayal still had to be in the back of his mind.

"I know I don't have a right to ask you this, Darcy, but please, help me find out what really happened. I need to find McKenzie and bring her home, now more than ever."

The way he looked at me triggered my sense of guilt and obligation. I had made that promise to him and he was collecting on it now. "Whatever happened, we'll figure it out together," I said.

"Thank you."

There wasn't much more we were going to figure out by sitting here speculating. Especially not when the victim's family was sitting down for a meal in the dining room. If there was any real motive to kill Sheila, they'd be more likely to shed light on it. I just had to be sure I could go digging without arousing too many suspicions.

"Come on, let's see what Tania made for dinner," I said and rose to my feet.

I led the way through the short foyer into the industrial kitchen and to the dining room. I knew that the table could seat a fair number of folks, but the space was positively crammed with people and bowls. An oversized crockpot of chili sat in the center of the table on a warmer.

"Serve yourself and find space where you can," Tania instructed as she crouched by Simon, trying to entice him to eat.

I ladled chili into a bowl and scanned the assembled strangers. I spotted Sheila's sister standing by the window overlooking the backyard. I moved to stand beside her. My hip bumped the small table that had once housed a large flowerpot filled with fake flowers and the drug money Vera had stolen from her ex-boyfriend.

"You were with the woman who died," I broached, not wanting to come off as knowing too much about this woman's business.

She turned and I spotted the red rims under her eyes. She'd been crying. Well, that was a good sign; it meant she was processing what happened. "My sister," she choked out. Her hands shook so violently that the spoon in her left hand rattled dangerously, threatening to spill the contents of her bowl on the floor.

"I'm so sorry. This must be such an awful day," I said.

"I knew we shouldn't have gone on the stupid trip," she continued, the proverbial floodgates opening up. "She said we needed to do something as couples. But she hates tours. She finds them dull as dirt. But she insisted we go on the cruise to this island."

"Maybe she was trying to get out of her comfort zone, or do something you liked?" I suggested.

She glanced over her shoulder at the family sitting at the table with her husband and brother-in-law both squished together at the far end of the table. "I think Trevor would have enjoyed it, that's her husband, but he's been glued to his phone since we met up yesterday."

"Did you tell her you didn't want to go?"

She shook her head. "No. I thought maybe for once she was right and it might be good for us. We hadn't seen each other in ages. But we were all just miserable. And if I'm being honest, I'm half-convinced she was planning to leave Trevor and just wanted someone to back her up."

None of that gave me any inclination as to why McKenzie might have tried to drown Sheila. Although, it seemed she might have had reason to go after Trevor. "Do you have any idea what might have happened? I saw her in the Tea Shoppe and she looked frightfully ill."

"She was complaining most of the trip to town about feeling sick to her stomach. I'd told her to take some medication before we got on the boat, but she didn't listen."

"Do you think she was looking for something to help her stomach?" I probed.

"I told her some tea might help." The woman's jaw dropped open. "You don't think the tea killed her?"

I hadn't seen her drink anything in our short interaction, but that didn't rule it out. In our brief exchange, Sheila had imparted she was waiting on an order.

"I don't mean to pry, but do you think Trevor had any idea she was planning to leave him?"

The woman let out a shrill laugh. "No. Sometimes I'm not even sure he remembers he has a wife ..." She paused, tears sparkling in her eyes. "H-had a wife."

I was sure Chief Hayes would have asked about his whereabouts this afternoon. From what I knew about police investigations, when someone died and they left behind a spouse, that person topped the suspect list until proven otherwise.

"However, it happened, I'm sorry for your loss," I offered. "I saw her at the tea shop. I was getting her some water when she went off toward the beach. Maybe if I had been faster, I don't know ... she might not have died."

The woman's face fell. "Oh, that was kind of you. I just don't understand how it could have happened. She wasn't near the water ..." Sheila's sister trailed off, retreating into her thoughts.

I focused on my food and downed it quickly. I retreated to the kitchen and found Sam sulking by the stove. He threw furtive glances toward the dining room and I turned on the water to cover my words.

"You can't have it both ways you know, wanting this place busy for Tania's sake and being gloomy, because they can't see you."

"I don't mind them, but you ignored me earlier."

"Sorry, a woman died and I'm trying to understand how it happened."

His eyes widened. "Trying to play detective, again?"

"McKenzie might be involved and Walter's asked for my help. I can't exactly refuse. If I can figure this out and reunite them, then he can go home."

Sam's face fell. "You don't have to be in such a hurry to get rid of him."

I snorted. "You realize he's alive, and not gay, right?"

"A ghost can dream," Sam answered just as Tania walked in balancing several empty bowls.

I plucked the first two off the pile and started to wash and rinse them. She fell in beside me to set them on the drying rack. "Thank you for being so accommodating."

"I am always happy to help those in need. But I did appreciate the slight heads up," Tania replied, accepting another bowl. "You really do seem to have some kind of luck with getting tangled up in things, don't you?"

"I don't try. Bad things seem to happen around me. I don't know, if McKenzie is somehow involved all of this, maybe I was meant to be on that boat today and so was Walter. Maybe this is the universe's way of finally helping me put this to rest so we can all move forward."

Tania nodded slowly. "It certainly seems like it might."

"Not that I have any idea how she fits in to all of this. The closest I can get to a motive is maybe the victim's husband suspected she might leave him, but that's not even definite."

"Well, I'm sure Rick and Vinnie will figure it out. Sometimes, deaths are accidents. For all we know, McKenzie was simply in the wrong place at the wrong time, if she was involved at all."

"Let's hope so. And let's also hope that they can discover what happened quickly, so that these people can get back to their lives, too."

In short order, the rest of the guests finished their meals and I helped Tania get them settled upstairs. She put Simon's family in the largest of the guest rooms and produced a twin mattress from the depths of the attic. Sheila's husband ended up in the room between mine and Walter's, while her sister and brother-in-law wound up across the hall. She'd put the captain in the room closest to the stairs, but he hadn't made his way upstairs yet. Last I saw, he'd been sitting in the kitchen away from everyone. Vinnie sat in the living room, nursing a mug of coffee. His phone sat on the arm of his chair and I could see a string of texts between him and Chief Hayes about Corinne living on the island. No need for her to come stay, then, especially as there hadn't appeared to be any other boats on the island when we'd left.

The day's events were catching up to me, but I wanted to know all I could. I sat down in one of the chairs facing him. "Has there been any word from Chief Hayes on what happens next?"

"Not yet. But we should be able to have these folks back home soon enough. Just have to check some things with the residents of the island."

He didn't elaborate, but I assumed he meant check for security cameras. It's not something I would typically imagine a small island to have. However, if the inhabitants were as wealthy as Corinne had indicated and given the amount of technology I'd seen in the server room, it made sense they would want to keep track of who came and went in their space.

What else might those cameras have picked up?

Keeping things to myself last time with Vera's case had caused unnecessary friction with the police and I had no desire to ruffle Chief Hayes' feathers again. "I don't know if the Chief told you, but there were reports of someone else near the body."

Vinnie fixed me with a tired look. "Kids are notoriously unreliable."

"I saw something like it, too. Well, not near the body, but as we were pulling into dock on the island. I saw someone in the water."

"Could have been one of the residents out for a swim."

"This was far out. I know the island isn't that far from shore here, but a twenty minute trip would take well beyond twice that to swim."

"So, you think what, a mermaid killed our victim?"

"No. Of course not. But I think it's worth looking into that someone not from the tour group might have been nearby."

Vinnie held up his mug. "I'm going to top up, excuse me."

As I retreated to my room, I tried to decide what my next step should be. Security footage could definitely shed light on things, but I had no reason to go looking for it and no one would turn it over to me.

And as much as I liked Beau's ability to camouflage me with his magic, I wasn't nearly tech savvy enough to break in and find the footage on my own.

Maybe some sleep would illuminate some new avenues. I curled up beneath the blankets and fell into a fitful sleep, chasing the answers that eluded me.

7

——————

I woke to the sound of soft knocks on my bedroom door. I rolled over and cracked one eye open, confused by the sound. Then, I remembered we had more guests with us than usual. That said, my vision resolved to reveal Walter standing in the doorway, fully dressed, and looking far more awake than anyone had a right to be at this hour.

"Come on, we need to go," he said in a hushed tone.

His words were enough to rouse me from my stupor. I sat up, scrubbed the last vestiges of sleep from my eyes and kicked off the blankets. "What's going on?"

"We need to go back to the island," he answered, as if it were perfectly logical.

"Um, if you couldn't find McKenzie yesterday, what makes you think you can find her today? Also, Corinne told me that no one gets on the island unless they've been verified by being with a tour company," I answered, rummaging in my closet for clean clothes.

"Honestly, I didn't have much time to look and if you're right and that little boy saw her on the beach near the dead body, then I was clearly looking in the wrong place."

I turned to face him and my heart skipped a beat. His face shone with such exuberance. He really believed this was going to work out. I hated to dash those hopes. "I've got to work today. But I'm off at three. If you can wait until then, I'll go with you."

Walter's face fell, but he nodded. "Oh, I understand. You can't just drop everything. And I guess this gives me time to figure out how we're getting back over there. I'll meet you on the pier at 3:30 then."

"I'll be there," I said and held up my clothes, a signal for some privacy.

He gave me a small smile before easing the door shut behind him. I tugged on fresh shorts and a brightly colored High Time shirt before trekking to the bathroom to get cleaned up. It was no surprise the rest of the B&B was quiet. After the day everyone had, they were all likely exhausted.

"You're snooping without me," Sam bemoaned, appearing in a wispy reflection in the mirror above the sink.

"I don't suppose you can make it out to the island?" I asked as I wrangled my curls into a knot on the top of my head.

Sam pouted. "Believe me, I've tried. I would love to see how those rich pricks live, but for some stupid reason I can't go beyond the boardwalk."

"Maybe ghosts can't cross bodies of water?" I suggested.

He shrugged before stopping mid-air to eye the room that Sheila's husband had occupied last night. The door sat ajar and I could make out the edge of an unmade bed. Perhaps Walter and I weren't the only ones up this early.

"You know, you might not be able to go to the island, but you do have one very big advantage here," I noted, taking the stairs as slowly as I could to prolong our conversation in privacy.

Sam's frown vanished, replaced by an eager grin. "I do love spying on people."

"You can't just go into their rooms while they're in there. But if you want to have a look around while they aren't there, that might be helpful."

"If I could touch things, I'd kiss you," he exclaimed and disappeared with a whoop, the sound echoing in my ears.

It probably wasn't the smartest move to have him go digging for information on other guests, but at least he couldn't leave fingerprints behind. And he really did just want to be a part of something.

I found Tania standing by the back window in the kitchen, staring out at a point on the horizon. I didn't disturb her as I got a cup of coffee. I made just enough noise for her to know someone else was in the room. She turned toward me.

"You're going to help Walter," she said in a hushed tone.

"I don't see how I can say no. I did promise the man I'd help him find his sister. And it certainly seems like something on that island points to her being there. And I still can't explain why there would be sea water on the body. McKenzie's water magic might hold the answers, but I've only got a shot at finding those if we can find her."

"Just be careful. You don't want to get wrapped up in things you shouldn't."

"Believe me, I have no desire to get on Chief Hayes' bad side. But I also can't shake that there is something odd going on," I replied.

"Just be careful," Tania repeated and stepped away from the window. She made a beeline for the stove, pulling out pans, and setting them on burners.

"Need help?" I offered, but she shooed me away.

"I appreciate that, but no."

I vacated the kitchen and moved through the empty dining room to the small living room with its chairs and couch. I hadn't seen Vinnie yet this morning, although I spotted the rumple of the couch cushions that suggested someone had laid on them. I don't know why he would have felt compelled to sleep down here when Tania had plenty of unoccupied rooms to spare.

Sheila's husband occupied one of the chairs, his hand loosely grasping his cell phone. His expression was blank, as if he had never felt an emotion in his life. My foot caught the edge of the rug, sending me stumbling into the back of the second chair. It was enough to pull the man from his stupor.

"Sorry," I mumbled, grateful I'd managed not to spill my coffee all over the chair.

"I forgot there were other people here," he said.

I knew shock and trauma could do strange things

to a person's memory, but even with Simon and his sibling sleeping upstairs, I had been acutely aware that there were lots of people in this house. He eyed my coffee and then looked at the darkened screen of his phone.

"I can go if you need to make a personal call," I said.

The man shook his head. I only now recalled his name was Trevor. "I don't know who I'd call."

I settled in the chair opposite him and cupped my mug between my hands. "Do you have parents you'd need to notify?"

"Both sets of our parents are dead. We never had kids. It's just me and Rachel and Bryan."

I assumed those were his sister and brother-in-law. He had no need to tell them about what had happened. "I'm sure you can take a day or two to wrap your head around things while the police investigate. You don't have to rush into anything."

"I just ... I didn't want to go on the cruise. I'm not outdoorsy and she knew that. At least I thought she did," he answered.

That tracked with what Rachel had shared last night about Sheila's personality. But it didn't explain why she would drag her family out to an island when none of them would have enjoyed it. In fact, they hadn't appeared to enjoy being in each other's company at all.

"Could she have been trying to, I don't know, spice things up?"

Trevor let out a strangled laugh. "Nothing like that had been going on in months. I thought maybe it was just hormone changes or what have you. That maybe that's why she'd lost interest. But it was very unlike her to suggest this trip."

"Had she been acting strangely otherwise before the trip?" I probed.

"I'd been working long hours on some projects at work. Summer is our busy season. I thought it was just the usual missing each other, because I got home so late. But she was up and out of the house sometimes before I woke up."

"Where'd she go?"

"I have no idea. I was just trying to pretend nothing was wrong between us and ignored it. I figured, if I didn't acknowledge it, then it wasn't really happening." He set his phone in his lap and buried his head in his hands. "If I'd tried more in my marriage, would she still be alive?"

I couldn't answer his question, but it did pose a new line of inquiry. If Sheila had been acting strangely the last few months and this trip really was not something she'd have done before, then how had she found out about it? And why bring her family along for the ride? Why had her sister thought Sheila was going to leave her husband? All questions I'd have to consider while I tended plants at work.

"I'm really sorry all of this is happening," I said.

"Thank you," he murmured and went back to staring at his blank phone screen.

I downed the rest of my coffee and stopped in the kitchen long enough to grab a breakfast burrito Tania had whipped up for me as she made omelettes for everyone else before leaving the house. I found Vinnie standing sentinel on the front porch, his uniform shirt rumpled. He caught me before I could make it past the first step.

"Chief Hayes wants folks to stay here," he said.

"Well, you can tell the Chief that I've got a job to go to and if he needs to talk to me, he knows where to find me," I replied.

Vinnie's shoulders sank a little. "I guess that's fine."

"Tania's making omelettes in there. I think she's got one with your name on it" I told him.

He brightened and turned on his heel to head inside. He stopped with his hand on the handle when his phone rang. I started down the steps, straining to hear what might be communicated to him when he answered.

"Morning, Chief," Vinnie greeted.

I couldn't make out Chief Hayes on the other end of the line, but I glanced over my shoulder to find Vinnie frowning.

"It's an island. It's not like there are a lot of places to hide."

Who is he talking about? McKenzie, or someone else?

"No, sir. I understand. I'll wait here while you head back and try to find her. I can run a background check and send you what I find. I'm sure she had to get a permit to build her shop."

I hurried down the driveway and onto the sidewalk, so Vinnie didn't think I was lingering or eavesdropping. From what I could gather, they were having trouble finding Paula, the Tea Shoppe's proprietor. Vinnie was right, it was difficult to lose someone on an island.

As I walked the familiar path to work, I resolved to do what digging I could into Sheila. If I could understand who she was, then maybe I might have a chance of figuring out how she had ended up dead on that island.

8

———

*D*espite the trauma of the day before, High Time's break room was surprisingly lively when I walked in. I could tell by the looks of shock on some of my co-workers faces, they'd heard the news and probably some details they shouldn't know. Though Sage wasn't halting the gossip, yet.

"I didn't get a chance to tell you, I thought you were really brave, taking charge like that yesterday," Thomas said, pulling me aside before I could make my way into the growth room.

"I did what anyone would do," I protested, eager to be in the relative solitude my position entailed.

Thomas pointed to himself. "I froze up. We all did. It was just so insane."

"Are you sure you didn't see anything? I heard that little boy say he saw someone near the woman before she died," I probed.

Thomas' cheeks darkened and he averted his gaze. "I was a little preoccupied."

He mimed smoking a joint and I nodded. It didn't surprise me that some of the staff who worked here were also customers. I'd never asked Sage, but I would assume she'd offer some sort of discount.

"I should get to work," I noted and gestured to the door leading from the break room to the growth room.

"Yeah, me too." Thomas tucked a few errant dreadlocks up into his hairnet before returning to his station.

Getting information from my co-workers would have been simple, and helpful, but that seemed too easy. I eased the door to the growth room shut and settled on the stool by the newest rows of seedlings. I'd grown accustomed to the scent the leaves gave off. When I'd first started here, it had been distracting, but now it was almost comforting. For all I knew, working here was giving me a contact high.

Knowing I couldn't just sit around and snoop on strangers all day, I tended to the plants first. I talked to each plant individually, pouring a little magic into each until I felt them stir and grow just a little. One day, maybe I'd be able to hold sway over a plant without having to touch it. At least that's what Tania assured me was possible. I was nowhere near that level, not yet anyway.

I moved to the tallest of the plants in the room. It had already been harvested a few times over. It was nearly at the end of its life and I could feel it's sense of impending sadness. It didn't want to die.

"I know it seems scary, mate," I said softly, propping my chin in one hand. "But you've had a fulfilling life and helped loads of people. You couldn't ask for more from a medicinal plant."

The plant's leaves unfurled a little and caressed my fingertips. I felt it shiver beneath my touch and did what I could to ease its uncertainty. Closing my eyes, I conjured up an image of a seedling, watching it grow tall and strong, offering up a bountiful harvest before withering and returning to the soil to give new life to future plants. It was the natural cycle. Nothing to be afraid of. When I opened my eyes, I found the stalk had drooped, draping over my hand as if the plant had succumbed to its end. I started to pull my hand away when the leaves turned brittle and the stalk crumbled beneath my hand. It fell into the soil, sinking in of its own accord.

Did I do that?

I turned the soil in the pot over and set it on the seedling tray, ready to receive a new life tomorrow. I was rather pleased with myself, if I had in fact been able to show the plant what was to come and aid it on its journey.

"Good on you, Darcy," I praised myself before sitting back in the chair and retrieving my phone.

That felt like a decent enough time spent tending the plants. I could do a little light Facebook surveillance on Sheila. I had her name half-typed into the Search bar when I realized I had no idea if she was actually on the platform. My finger hovered over the backspace button for a moment before I pushed forward and finished typing her name.

Only a couple of Sheila Bartows showed up in the search and one listed herself as still in college in California. *Probably not the right one.* I double tapped the profile image of the other Sheila and was rewarded with an image of Sheila and Trevor on what appeared to be their wedding day. They were about a decade younger in the photo, but I still recognized them. The looked so in love; not at all how Rachel or Trevor had described the relationship.

"Let's see why your sister thought you were going to leave your husband," I whispered and started to scroll through her profile. It was thankfully set to Public. I spotted only Rachel among her immediate family listed. Either Trevor wasn't on the platform or they just weren't friends. I guess that was one way to conceal your activities from your spouse. I found recent posts from Sheila, mostly quoting religious passages. I didn't recognize any of them. Skimming earlier posts revealed that her faith was not newly discovered, so that didn't offer any help. The photos she'd posted were mostly of nature and at gatherings with a whole host of names tagged—likely friendly get-togethers. I enlarged a few of the photos with Sheila and other people. It didn't look like she was standing inexplicably close to anyone other than Trevor. I did notice that she looked less happy as time passed, moving toward the present. Her smile was more tight-lipped and forced. That didn't mean anything in particular, but it did seem consistent. I flipped back to the last photo where she looked truly happy. It was at some event tagged as 'Marsha's 50th.'" Whoever had taken photos at the event had a real eye for documenting candid moments. Sheila was in several of the shots, laughing and engaged with the people around her. This party had been four months ago.

"What happened four months ago, Sheila?" I wondered aloud just as the door to the growth room opened behind me.

"Hey, some folks are going to Ginny's for lunch. Want to come?" Thomas asked.

"Yeah, I'll come. Thanks," I replied and followed him back through the kitchen to a waiting cluster of other employees. The fact that those assembled were most of the contingent from the cruise didn't escape my notice.

We moved in a tight knot across the street and into the diner. I didn't know how we were going to find space for everyone, but we ended up claiming two of the larger booths on the far side of the establishment. I spotted Ginny supervising from her usual perch at the counter. I also noted that Captain Merchant sat a few seats down from Ginny. Had Vinnie allowed people to leave the B&B after all or had the captain snuck off without permission?

I watched Captain Merchant as he stared at his phone, a scowl on his lips. I doubted he would know anything new, but I hoped I was wrong. Sparing a quick glance at our table, I noticed we lacked a bottle of ketchup. A spare one sat conveniently to the captain's right. It wasn't elegant, but it was pretense enough to make conversation. I left the booth and my co-workers behind, and closed the short distance to the counter.

"Excuse me," I said, tapping the man on the shoulder.

He jumped, his phone clattering to the surface in front of him. I caught a glimpse of some sort of ledger before he hit the power button, turning the screen black.

"Can I help you?" his voice was gruffer than it had been the day before.

"Sorry, I was just hoping to get that bottle of ketchup," I said, gesturing to the red container.

"I'm not using it," he answered, passing it over.

"Has there been some development with the woman who died yesterday?" I settled onto the raised stool beside him, twirling the bottle between my fingers

"What? Why would you ask that?"

"I was on the cruise and when I was leaving this morning, the officer told me that the Chief of Police wanted folks to stay put. Since you're here and not at the B&B, I thought maybe something had changed."

"Oh ..." The corner of his mouth twitched,

making the bushy beard quiver. "Haven't heard anything. But the officer didn't seem to mind me getting a bite to eat and a decent cup of coffee."

I bit back a retort about Tania's coffee being the superior brew. Instead, I tried to ingratiate myself. "This whole situation must be so frustrating. I couldn't imagine being in your position with it affecting my business."

"Not ideal," he offered in a tight-lipped response. He glanced down at his phone again as it buzzed with an incoming call. Without preamble, he scooped it up and stepped out of the diner.

I wanted to chalk his gruff demeanor up to the shock of losing one of his passengers in such a strange manner, but my gut told me that wasn't the case. None of this made sense. The bell above the door tinkled with a new patron. I turned to see Chief Hayes enter, approaching Ginny.

"You never come see me during a shift," Ginny noted as she greeted her brother.

"Man's got to eat," he answered as one of the wait staff appeared with a to-go bag. "This has been a weird one. Never seen prints in such unusual places before."

Oh, how I wished I had Beau's invisibility power right now. It would make listening in on their conversation so much simpler. His statement conjured up an image of Sheila's body covered in fingerprint powder. I wondered what constituted unusual. Ginny turned on her stool, our gazes meeting for a split second. I had no real reason to remain at the counter and retreated back to my table. I busied myself pretending to look over the menu before placing my order. I kept the Chief in my peripheral vision.

"Just let me know if you hear anything," Chief Hayes addressed Ginny.

"I'd say it isn't my job, but you know I love you. So, I'll do what I can," Ginny answered.

Was he using her truth-seeking abilities to his advantage? Could he really be willing to use his own sister in an investigation when he treated me as a suspect when I did the same thing? I guess blood really was thicker in some cases.

"I don't need this right now!" Captain Merchant's voice boomed as Chief Hayes exited the diner.

Whatever conversation he'd been having ended when the Chief approached him. I could just make out the captain sliding his phone back in his pocket as he conversed with Chief Hayes. Something had definitely agitated the man, but I couldn't imagine what.

I could barely focus on my food. There was so much to consider and to pass along to Walter. I had no doubt he'd have some ideas about what all of this could mean. I just hoped he'd managed to get us passage back to the island and that whatever awaited us there brought some much needed answers.

9

By the time the end of my shift came, I was pacing the length of the growth room like a caged wild animal. I might not have started out intending to solve this mystery, but now that I was in it, I couldn't get it out of my head. I knew the pieces had to fit together, but it was like trying to put it together without knowing what the final product was meant to be. I ran to the board-walk, scanning every face until I saw Walter waiting by a small motorboat. It bobbed low in the water and my stomach did a flip. I'd handled the cruise ship okay with the help of Maggie's concoction, but the difference in size and my proximity to the water had been a deciding factor.

"You couldn't have chartered something bigger?" I rasped.

"I know you aren't big on boats, but this was the best I could find on short notice. No one is really going out to the island now that someone's died there. I had to pay triple the rental fee for this boat just to secure it and get the owner to give me a manifest for two passengers."

"Word spreads fast," I noted.

"Come on, we're wasting daylight."

I should have gone back to the clinic for more of Maggie's potion, but Walter grabbed my wrist and hauled me aboard. The motor droned too loudly to hold a conversation, which was probably safer. It allowed me to focus on regulating my breathing and not lose my lunch over the side of the boat. Our speed increased at the midway point and the choppiness seemed to smooth, giving me a small reprieve.

"Hang on," Walter called and slowed the boat. He climbed out, up to his ankles in water as he dragged the boat ashore.

I clamored over the side until my feet were firmly on the dry sand and I bent double to catch my breath and steady my balance. *I really hate boats.* "How'd you know how to do all of this?"

"Boy Scouts. Years and years at summer camp. Some things stick with you," he replied with a proud grin.

I expected Corinne to appear in her stilettos to greet us or demand to know why we're intruding on her space again. After all, from the text I'd spied on Vinnie's phone, she lived here. She was nowhere to be seen and I made a mental note of that.

"So, I checked down that end of the beach yesterday and found nothing to indicate anyone was living out here. So maybe we head the opposite direction," Walter said, practically bouncing on the balls of his feet.

"Sure. But there's some things we need to consider," I said and started up the beach at a leisurely pace.

"Like what?'

"I overheard Vinnie this morning on the phone with Chief Hayes. They can't find the Tea Shoppe's owner. It seemed like it was a big deal."

"Maybe they are just trying to make sure they get everyone's statements," Walter offered.

I shook my head and wiped beads of sweat from my upper lip. "She was missing when they were rounding everyone up. And I know that Sheila was waiting for something in her shop when we crossed paths."

"Okay, so that is a little suspicious."

"There's more. I may have been eavesdropping at Ginny's, but Chief Hayes also mentioned that they found fingerprints in an unusual place on Sheila's body. I have no idea what that means and he asked Ginny to let him know if she heard anything."

"He never struck me as the kind of person to solicit civilian help."

"Certainly not in my experience," I grumbled. "And then there's the digging I did into Sheila's social media. Her sister thought she was leaving her husband, but nothing there suggests it. But I did notice that something changed about four months back. She just looked less happy."

"That could be anything," Walter sighed.

"I know." I picked up the pace enough to block Walter's way forward. "What happens if we find McKenzie?"

"We bring her back with us."

"If she's been hiding out here the whole time, what makes you think she'd just come back with us? You keep saying she knows you're here, and yet she hasn't come looking for you. Even if we do find her, I doubt she's going to want to come with us."

"I know I can convince her to come. I just need to talk to her and explain things."

I envied his optimism that everything would simply work out. Maybe he was just trying to convince himself of that fact since the journey to get this far had been so rocky, relying on the kindness and observant nature of strangers to point him in the right direction.

"We better start looking. I don't like being here without anyone knowing where we went. For all we know, it could have been someone who lives on the island that attacked Sheila," I said and spun back the way we'd been walking.

I scanned the sand for any hint of someone taking up prolonged residence, yet there was nothing. *Of course, there wouldn't be, you bloody idiot!* We're too close to the ocean. The tide would have come and washed anything away.

"I think we ought to move inland," I said and pointed for the tree line

The beach sloped up toward the greenery and I had to tug my feet free of the sand, as if the latent moisture in it was trying to trap me. We reached the tree line and I stopped, palm resting on one of the tree trunks to dust sand out of my pants.

"Can you sense her?"

Walter closed his eyes and his brow furrowed. "It's there. She's nearby, but I can't get a direction. I don't know, maybe because she knows what my power is, she's somehow able to deflect it."

I wondered if ghosts weren't the only supernatural creatures stymied by water. If McKenzie had learned to control her power over time, what was to say she couldn't defend against other magic? The bark of the tree beneath my hand warmed.

"I might have a way of finding her," I said with a grin.

Walter took a step back to give me space to work and I pressed both hands to the tree. "I know we've never met before, but I need your help. We need to find a woman who's been here. She's not supposed to be here, she doesn't belong among you. Please, can you show us where to look?"

I closed my eyes and pictured McKenzie from her Facebook photos with Walter—her dark hair and eyes. The bark grew hot against my skin and I pulled my palms off, afraid I was about to ignite the wood. As quickly as it had heated, it cooled and tension ebbed from between my shoulder blades. With my eyes still squeezed shut, I tried to summon the mental image of my magic in action, but it wasn't there. Instead, I could see a thick stand of trees stretched out in front of me. I could feel a breeze blow across my neck from right to left. Like someone had filmed through the trees and then sped it up double time, I mentally zipped through the foliage until I found a small hut that could have been an abandoned shed or maybe the quarters of a care-taker on one of the secluded properties.

"I know where to look." My words were too loud in my ears as the connection to the trees dissipated.

"That was amazing," Walter said as I led him through the trees in the direction of the hut.

"I asked them to help and they did," I explained. The path was as clear to me now as it had been in the vision I'd shared with the trees.

Up until this point I'd only been trying to commune with smaller plants and flowers. I'd even tried getting the grass in the backyard to grow. That had been a waste of energy. But the trees had been more than willing to offer an assist. That was encouraging.

I held up a hand to stop Walter from charging forward when the hut came into view. Even if it wasn't legally hers, this had served as McKenzie's hiding place for a while now. For all intents and purposes this was her home and she had a right to not be caught off guard.

The plants around the hut bristled even though there was no breeze to speak of. It was a warning that made my arms tingle and my teeth ache. Whatever we were about to walk into, it wasn't friendly.

"You should temper your expectations," I told Walter as a chorus of tiny voices shouted in my head. *Danger!*

The door to the hut swung outward and I held my breath, bracing for whatever came next. Walter stepped up; hands held so whoever waited could see them.

"We just want to talk, Kenz."

The thrum of the plants in my head rose to a deafening buzz. The ground shook beneath our feet and my ears ached at a sudden change in the air pressure around us. I had just enough time to shout, "Walter look out!" before a towering wave crashed through the trees, sweeping us up in its current and carrying us back toward the beach. Just before the trees hid the hut from view, I saw McKenzie standing in the doorway her hand outstretched.

She was more powerful than I'd anticipated.

Bugger.

10

The wave receded, leaving Walter and I halfway back to the beach. I shivered as the water glistened on my skin and I tasted salt on my tongue. Walter staggered against a tree beside me.

"Did you know she could do that?" I demanded.

Walter sputtered and shook his head. "No, I swear. The last time I saw her, she was doing little things; controlling small amounts of water for a few seconds. Nothing like that."

The direct assault certainly suggested that McKenzie wasn't happy to see her big brother. Maybe all these months alone had made her paranoid that he wasn't on her side.

"Let me try talking to her," I suggested and

started back through the tree line before he could protest.

The trees were still on my side and parted, branches bending to signal the way as I went. I didn't want to fight, but I wasn't about to let this woman push me around. She wasn't the only one with an elemental connection on this island. I made it back to the hut to find the door still open, but McKenzie had vanished.

I wasn't about to go into this unprepared. For one thing, I'd never actually used my magic in a defensive way before. Not consciously anyhow. I wasn't a great judge of distance, but the wave McKenzie had summoned could have come from a good ten to twenty feet away. I knew I didn't have that kind of reach, but I wasn't without support. The trees murmured in my head, as if pledging their loyalty to me.

"McKenzie, my name's Darcy. I just want to talk to you. I'm not here to hurt you, I promise."

I felt the ground rumble before I heard the rush of water. The wave came crashing through the trees and knocked me off my feet, pulling me under. I had just enough time to suck in a breath so I wouldn't drown. The salty taste still hit my lips and it triggered my fear of water, sending my heart hammering in my chest. I groped blindly around me until my fingers found the rough bark of a nearby tree. I hoped the connection could somehow keep me grounded. The water receded and I gasped for air. Tiny black spots popped in my vision and dizziness threatened to topple me.

My ears picked up the rushing sound of another onslaught and I bit back a growl of frustration. I moved my hand up to a low-hanging branch and clamped on. To my surprise, tiny tendrils of green sprouted from where my palm made contact, looping around my wrist. It cinched tight against my skin just enough to hold me steady when the water came crashing through. At least she seemed to only have one trick up her sleeve.

"Oy! I really don't appreciate getting drenched here," I shouted trying not to let the chill of my damp clothes make my teeth chatter.

"Go away!"

I wasn't about to let her soak me again. Time to do a little offensive magic. McKenzie stepped out into the doorway again, hands raised. The vines around my wrist receded, allowing me to step forward as I closed the distance.

"I'm not leaving until we've had a chat. You know something about that woman's death yesterday."

I anticipated the next wave and reached out to the trees around me. *I know it's not fair, but I need you to shield me*, I thought. And they did. Foliage reached out, stretching beyond their limits to deflect the deluge. The effort and connection seemed to crash over me as a metaphorical wave and I stumbled.

"Look, I understand if you don't want to talk to your brother. Family is complicated. But I'm not the police. I'm just a lass from London who can do things with plants like you can with water. I just want to help," I called.

McKenzie's hands lowered and she seemed to sag with the weight of the battle of wills like I'd done. Maybe she wasn't as powerful as I'd thought. She gestured for me to enter the hut and I followed her in. It was a single room with a sagging mattress on the floor and there wasn't even a toilet.

"How long have you been here?" I probed softly.

"I don't know, a few weeks," she answered, keeping her distance.

"You know there's a perfectly good bed and breakfast in town."

"I can't see him." McKenzie's shoulders hunched until they were practically touching her ears.

"Who, Walter? Love, he's not mad at you if that's

what you're worried about. He's been beside himself if I'm honest."

McKenzie's gaze widened. "You're sure?"

"He's been relying on the kindness of strangers pointing him your way. He just wants to help. And apologize for pushing you too fast."

Her shoulders lowered a little, but the tension slipped down her arms and into her hands. She kneaded her fingers together and began to pace. "I don't think I'm ready to go home. There's too much there that feels like pressure and expectations."

"I understand. Magic is still pretty new for me, too. But it shouldn't be something you're afraid of. It's a part of you for a reason."

"But no one bothers me here," she said, unclasping her hands to gesture to the meager surroundings.

"Maybe not, but you can't be happy living out here alone without basic amenities. Come back to Brookhaven with us. Have a hot shower, a warm meal, and a decent bed."

"That does sound nice."

"Brilliant. Let's get going then. And maybe on the way, you could fill us in on what you know about what happened yesterday."

I marched out of the hut, retracing my path to

the beach. I found Walter pacing in the sand, glancing toward the tree line behind us furtively. Had Corinne or one of the residents spotted us? I was honestly surprised we hadn't seen the stiletto-clad woman since arriving.

"She's coming back with us," I announced.

He startled, his movements jerky and awkward as he faced me. "Thank ..." he trailed off, craning his neck to peer behind me. "Where is she?"

I made a quarter turn to find the path behind me empty. I could have sworn McKenzie had been following me back to the beach. I let out an involuntary groan and a shiver as a gust of wind blew past, reminding me just how wet my clothes were. Anger cascaded over me from head to foot and I whipped around. I was not leaving this bloody island without McKenzie.

I wasn't sure how it happened, but a thick vine erupted from the beach at my feet. It slithered snake-like into the trees. I heard an audible yelp and some colorful cursing as the vine retreated, dragging McKenzie around the middle.

"It isn't very nice to say you'll come along and then bail," I noted when the vine deposited her at my feet.

She glared up at me as the vine unwound itself

from her torso and looped around her wrist. The other end of the vine slid up my palm and secured itself around my own wrist. I let her give it a firm tug, but it didn't break. Even when she tried to bite it, all she came away with were tiny cuts on her lips.

"We're going back to town and you're telling us what you know," I declared. To Walter I said, "Get the boat, please."

He took off at a sprint and I waited there, bound to the woman who held answers to the mystery that had befallen this island. She looked miserable as we waited for Walter and the boat, and I couldn't' help feeling sorry for her. Though not sorry enough to let her go, mind you.

When the boat appeared just beyond the depth where it would beach itself, I tugged McKenzie to her feet and ushered her into the boat.

"Right, now no more tricks. You try to dive over the side or capsize us, and we're all dead," I noted.

"Got it," McKenzie murmured.

I was so determined to keep her in check that I didn't pay much attention to the trip back across the water. I suspected my warning in combination with the exertion from our little tiff had worn McKenzie out enough to keep her powers in check.

We reached the boardwalk and Walter leapt up

to secure the boat. I helped McKenzie onto land and the tiny hairs on the nape of my neck bristled. I turned and spotted Sam's translucent form first, followed by Tania and Chief Hayes.

That's not good.

The Chief charged at us, a look of pure disdain on his face. "What part of staying put did you not understand?" he barked at me.

"We came back," I noted.

"With a new face," Tania interjected.

"My sister," Walter said.

"You're McKenzie Lawson?" Chief Hayes eyed McKenzie with a hard expression.

"Yes," McKenzie tugged at the vine securing us together.

She wasn't likely to run if the police were talking to her, so I let the vine recede. She rubbed at her wrist and kept her gaze focused on a spot around the chief's navel. I caught Tania arch a brow at me and I offered a silent shrug.

"Ms. Lawson, you're going to need to come with me," Chief Hayes said.

"What? Why?" Walter moved to place himself between the Chief and his sister.

"Because she is a person of interest in Sheila Bartow's death."

11

———

I gaped at the Chief as he took McKenzie by the wrist and led her up the board-walk. She cast a plaintive look my way as she passed Tania. We'd clearly missed something during our excursion back to the island.

"What's happened?" I addressed Tania.

"I heard him tell the cute cop that they rushed fingerprints on the body and that McKenzie Lawson's prints were on her face," Sam reported with an almost gleeful lilt to his voice.

Tania let out a sigh and restated the information for Walter's benefit. "Apparently there was some new evidence that points to your sister."

I could understand now why the chief wanted to speak to her. It certainly looked bad if her fingerprints were on a dead woman's body. Especially when it appeared that the dead body had drowned.

Walter opened his mouth to speak and no doubt proclaim his sister's innocence when I held up a hand to silence him. "We have no evidence to believe McKenzie would have wanted to harm Sheila."

Sam gestured to my water-logged clothing. "Guessing water witch did that."

"Yeah, McKenzie sent a few waves our way," I said, translating Sam's quip for Walter.

"She was just scared," Walter protested.

"And the fact that we're a sopping mess and Sheila wasn't suggests to me that she has more control over her power. I would think if she'd really wanted to hurt us, she would have made the waves more targeted."

"So, what do we do now?" The strain in Walter's tone betrayed his anxiety.

"We go back to the B&B. I need dry clothes."

I also wanted to check with Sam in private to see if he had any success in his snooping on the other cruise participants. Tania, Walter, and I walked three abreast back to the B&B. Vinnie was no longer stationed on the front steps.

"Chief Hayes sent him home to get some rest. He's sending over a temporary officer from a nearby town in about an hour" Tania explained. "The rest of our guests are settling in for an early dinner."

Food sounded heavenly, but a change of clothes was in order first. I raced up the stairs two at a time and turned into my room to find Sam waiting for me. Beau perched on my pillow. I bent down and gave the chameleon a stroke along his back.

"Do you want to know what I found out?" If Sam had been able to stand on the floor, he would have bounced right off it with the exuberance that wafted from him.

"I do, but I've got to get these wet things off first." I gestured to the door. "I don't need an audience."

"Nothing I haven't seen before," Sam snorted, but vanished.

I pushed that disturbing image from my mind and gathered fresh clothes before retreating to the bathroom. The shivers that still ran through my body told me a hot shower was also in order. Ten minutes later I stepped out, feeling more human.

Returning to my room, Sam reappeared. "Well, I will admit, drowned rat isn't really a good look on you, so changing was a good call."

"Glad I no longer offend you," I retorted. "Now, what have you learned?"

"Well, her husband spent four hours glued to his phone."

"That's nothing new. He was on his phone all during the trip yesterday, too."

"Yeah, well I don't know what he was looking at yesterday, but today he kept scrolling through bank statements."

"So? He's got to plan a funeral for his wife. It's not like they're cheap. For all we know he was just making sure he had enough money to do it."

"And I overheard him talking to his bank trying to dispute a whole bunch of charges over the last four months."

Now, that sounded promising. Four months ago, there had been a change in Sheila's presence and demeanor on social media. Had Trevor actually found some evidence that Sheila was sneaking around behind his back and planning to leave him?

"Could you figure out what the charges were for?"

"No idea. He kept reading off some name like tee-show or something. But they were big charges. Hundreds of dollars' worth. Two to three times a month."

The name took a minute to register. "Could it have been an abbreviation for the Tea Shoppe?"

Sam shrugged. "How should I know?" After a beat, his smirked. "You know, I have to admit I'm impressed our little hedge witch had the balls to drag another witch back with magic."

"Yeah, well, to be honest I'm not entirely sure how I managed it. And she walloped me good, too."

Sam spun in mid-air. "Anyway, the sister and brother-in-law just sort of sat around looking mopey.

That wasn't surprising. I doubted Rachel would have said anything outright to her brother-in-law without proof that Sheila had intended to leave him. Stoking rumors wasn't helpful. But the banking information Sam had uncovered raised the renewed question of what had happened to Paula, the reclusive shop owner? As much as I hated to admit it, I had another boat trip in my future.

I glanced to Beau who still sat perched on my pillow, blinking slowly. "You have any insights you'd like to offer?"

'Find Paula.'

"Trust me, that's on the list." I don't know why she would have been purchasing large quantities of tea from someone on a remote island. And what did it have to do with Sheila's sudden change in behavior?

That wasn't the only question that needed answering. Walter and I needed to know what McKenzie knew about Sheila's death. My instincts told me she knew more than any of us, even if she didn't think she did.

"Beau, mate, you up for a little trip?" I offered my arm as I spoke.

"Where are you going?" Sam interjected.

"On a little investigative mission," I answered and left the room.

I stopped two doors down and knocked, but received no response. I had assumed Walter would have wanted to get cleaned up, too, but maybe he'd already done so and was down eating with everyone else.

"I don't need people asking questions about you right now, so would you mind blending in?" I addressed the reptile as I descended the stairs.

I felt a ripple of magic dance up my arm as Beau blended himself into my arm. It was one of the more useful forms of magic I'd encountered since moving to town. I wasn't above using his particular skillset when it suited me and if he allowed it. Sure, I didn't like sneaking around, but sometimes it couldn't be helped. I found Walter pacing in the living room in dry clothes.

"Should I get her a lawyer?" he asked when he saw me.

"Being a person of interest doesn't mean she's a suspect. And even if she were, I'm sure they'd inform her of that and she would be smart enough to wait for one before she talked to them," I reassured him. "And if it makes you feel better, we can go down and watch the Chief question her."

Walter's eyes widened. "There is no way we'd be able to be in the room. I'm not a lawyer and last I checked, neither are you."

"I didn't say we'd be in the room. I have a way of slipping in unnoticed. Come on, we'd better get going before we miss everything."

"How are you going to manage that?" Walter asked as I ushered him to the front steps. Just as Tania had noted, a uniformed officer approached from the driveway. Good, they could see us and include us in the head count if Chief Hayes asked.

"Evening," the officer greeted in a melodious alto tone. She took off a pair of sunglasses and stowed them in her front pocket.

"Good evening. You must be Vinnie's replacement that the Chief sent over," I said and offered my non-reptile-bearing arm's hand. "I'm Darcy. This is

Walter. Everyone else is still sitting down for dinner."

"Good to meet you. I trust you two weren't on your way out just now."

"No ma'am," Walter said, entering the conversation.

"You really ought to come in and have a bite to eat. Tania, she runs this place, is an excellent cook," I boasted.

"I could eat," the officer replied. We led her through the foyer into the kitchen and the dining room.

Tonight's meal was two roast chickens with ample sides of potatoes and steamed vegetables. Tania spotted the new arrival and moved to greet her, explaining the buffet-style system. I packed a chicken thigh and some potatoes onto a plate and moved to stand off to one side, eating hurriedly. Walter did the same. The sooner we could slip away, the better.

'Through the kitchen,' I heard Beau's voice in my head.

Tania had moved to block the officer's view to the kitchen and I signaled for Walter to follow me. I carried the now-empty plate into the kitchen and set it in the sink, rinsing the residue off. I took Walter's plate too, before whispering, "Back door."

He darted to the back entrance and eased it open. After shutting off the tap, I followed him, casting one last glance over my shoulder to find Tania nodding and smiling.

'Go now.'

I wasn't going to argue with Beau. I pulled the door shut behind us and together Walter and I made our way to the police station. I knew from my past run-ins with Chief Hayes that the station housed a single bullpen, his office, a holding cell, a long hall that led to an evidence closet, and an interview room. That's where we'd find McKenzie.

Before we walked in, I grabbed Walter by the elbow. "We're going to have to stick really close together for this to work," I explained.

"For what to work?"

Beau momentarily shimmered out of existence on my arm, earning a gasp from Walter. I grinned. "Magical chameleons are pretty handy."

"What's going to happen?" He eyed me warily.

"Beau can camouflage himself and somehow he can extend that to other people, too."

"You've done this before, right?"

"Once or twice. It feels a bit odd at first, but you get used to it."

"I'm far less uncomfortable with this than I should be," he sighed. "Go ahead."

"You're up," I told Beau.

That strange co-mingling of heat and coolness wrapped itself around me as we took on the surrounding colors and textures of the world around us. It wasn't as disorienting for me this time as it had been before, but even hidden from view, I could still hear Walter's heavy breathing as he tried to calm his nausea. I waited a few seconds before starting forward into the station.

It was empty, a small blessing. I led the way down the hall to the interview room where we found Chief Hayes seated opposite McKenzie. She looked tired and kept wringing her hands together.

"I'm going to ask you again, Miss Lawson, how did your fingerprints wind up on a dead woman's body?"

"You think I hurt that woman. But I didn't ... I couldn't. I was just trying to help," McKenzie argued.

"Help? Help how?" The Chief leaned across the table that separated them.

"She was dying and I was just trying to save her."

12

─────────

I felt Walter's body relax beneath my grip. He'd insisted she wouldn't have killed anyone. I still didn't understand how she thought she had been helping this woman. Apparently, I wasn't alone.

"How do you know she was dying?"

"She was choking and I wanted to help. No one else was paying attention to her."

"If she was choking, why not try the Heimlich?" Chief suggested.

"I panicked."

"We found sea water in this woman's lungs. Can you explain that?"

McKenzie's body shifted in her seat and she

tugged a few strands of loose dark hair. "You wouldn't believe me."

"You'd be surprised what I can believe," the Chief replied.

"I ... I was trying to get her to throw up so she'd stop choking. It made sense in my head when I thought of it. But it went wrong. Maybe I was too late, but she just stopped breathing."

"Miss Lawson, the amount of water found in her lungs is consistent with drowning. She would have had to ingest a lot of water very quickly. You're saying you poured sea water into her mouth?"

"Well, not really poured. It was more like I wanted to get rid of whatever was inside her and the ocean went a little overboard."

"How did she wind up on the beach with dry clothing?"

"He's not going to believe her if she says magic," Walter hissed in my ears.

The Chief's body stiffened in the interview room and his head turned briefly in our direction before turning back to McKenzie, waiting for her response.

"He will," I whispered as low as I could.

"I had more control than I thought, but it wasn't enough," McKenzie answered.

From down the hall, I heard the front doors to

the station open and quick footsteps echoed on the floor. I craned my neck past Walter to see Vinnie racing toward the interview room. I pressed myself against the glass of the interview room just to avoid any possible collision and watched as Vinnie knocked once on the door to the room.

Chief Hayes stood and stepped out into the hall. "What is it?"

"We just got the toxicology report back."

That seemed fast. Surely it should have taken far longer than two days. Maybe they had a lab nearby that could run the results faster? Or maybe Chief Hayes had put a rush on it?

"She had poison in her blood. A lot of it," Vinnie continued. "And some other unidentified toxins. And her white blood cell count was off the charts."

Chief Hayes took the report from Vinnie's hand and studied it carefully. "I'll be done here in a few minutes. Wait for me and we'll go notify the husband. I think it's time he answered a few more questions."

Vinnie gave a curt nod and retreated to the front of the station. By the sound of wheels rolling across the floor, I guessed he'd taken up residence at his desk. Chief Hayes returned to the interview room where McKenzie still sat.

'*Calm,*' I heard Beau's voice. It was softer than normal, despite our close proximity.

McKenzie's shoulders slackened a little and I realized he'd been trying to ease her nerves. Chief Hayes settled back into his seat.

"Was there any strange smell when you approached the victim that prompted you to believe she was having trouble breathing?"

"Yes. It was strange. It was sort of nutty, but I couldn't put a name to it."

"Almonds?"

"I think so."

"So, let me understand. You smelled something like almonds on the victim, you saw she was in distress, and instead of calling 9-1-1, you chose to try and drown her in an effort to save her?"

"I didn't want to drown her. I honestly thought the water could help get her to throw up or something. And I don't have a phone. I lost it."

More like Vera had stolen it along with her ID. I waited for the Chief to press her on that unsolved interaction, but he made no mention of it. Apparently crossing paths with another dead woman weeks ago wasn't as important as solving the murder of the woman she'd met two days ago.

"For now, you are free to go, Miss Lawson. But you cannot leave town or return to Haven Island."

"So where am I supposed to go?" she protested.

"We have a perfectly good bed and breakfast that I believe your brother is acquainted with. I'll take you there."

I scurried back from the wall, dragging Walter with me. If Chief Hayes and Vinnie were on their way to Tania's to tell Trevor they'd found poison in his wife's blood, they would expect everyone to be there, including us. I shoved Walter into the open holding cell and waited long enough for Chief Hayes and McKenzie to walk by. The chief signaled for Vinnie to join them and they left the station.

"There is no way McKenzie poisoned that woman," Walter said when we left the station behind and the coast was clear.

"I believe you and I think so does the Chief. Even if there was some indication of drowning, I doubt he'd hold her fully responsible."

I wished Vinnie had told the Chief what sort of poison had been used. Even I knew that the smell of almonds meant cyanide. But I hadn't seen any evidence of almond plants when I'd been on the island the first time. Not that I'd been looking for them specifically. But already processed cyanide wasn't exactly something a normal person could get their hands on. Though maybe a reclusive tea shop owner might? It didn't explain why she would want Sheila dead or why Sheila had been making large purchases over the last few months. Besides, I hadn't actually seen them interact, so I had no confirmation that they'd even seen each other on the day of Sheila's murder.

"We need to find the tea shop owner," I declared as I ushered Walter back toward the B&B.

"What makes you think she's the one responsible?"

"I don't know that she is, but the fact that she's been missing since yesterday and not even the police can find her feels suspicious. If she's got nothing to hide, why keep yourself hidden?"

"Thank you for helping," he said as we ducked down the side of the B&B and back in through the kitchen.

"Not sure I've done much to help," I countered.

"You got her to come to back with us. I couldn't have done it on my own. If I'd tried, I probably would have wound up washed out to sea. But you convinced her. So, thank you."

"I'm just sorry she's mixed up in all of this, even if her intentions were noble."

"The truth will come out. I know it."

Tania appeared from the dining room carrying the last vestiges of dinner. "I hope your little adventure was useful," she said and set about stowing leftover food in containers. After a beat, her brow furrowed and she added, "I know it can be frustrating to feel like all you have is more questions."

"Uh, yes ... They're bringing McKenzie here. I'll go get a room set up for her," I said, leaving Walter and Tania in the kitchen.

Once upstairs, I took the time to check the other rooms. Simon and his family were curled up on the extra mattress and bed in their room. I caught Trevor pacing through the half open doorway to his room and heard low voices coming from Rachel and her husband's room. That left only Captain Merchant unaccounted for. I knew he'd insisted he didn't need to stay at the B&B, but surely he had to be somewhere on premises.

"Hey Sam?" I whispered.

"I don't like being summoned," the ghost responded, materializing at my elbow.

"Sorry, but I was trying to do a head count and I haven't seen the captain."

"That man took off as soon as he could. Not sure where he went, though."

Keeping track of him wasn't my problem. Except I made a mental note of the fact he wasn't present as I went about placing a set of towels on the bed in room 8 for McKenzie.

"What did you find spying on the police?" Sam's tone conveyed only mild interest.

"McKenzie probably isn't responsible for Sheila's death. But we still don't know who is or why they'd want her dead. The police did find something in her blood."

As if on cue, I heard the front door open and Chief Hayes' voice telling his other officer that he needed to speak with Trevor. She indicated that he was upstairs and I stepped into the room meant for McKenzie. He didn't need to see me snooping. I could also make out Tania's voice telling McKenzie there was still food leftover, but that she was welcome to just go upstairs and get cleaned up first. Based on the two sets of footsteps on the stairs, I assumed she was taking Tania up on the offer. Sure enough, McKenzie trailed Chief Hayes into the hallway.

"Your room is here," I said, stepping into the hall.

The Chief eyed me with suspicion. "We got it ready assuming she'd be coming back to stay," I answered the unasked question.

"Where can I find Trevor Bartow?"

I pointed to Trevor's room and left him to his business, ushering McKenzie into her room. "How are you holding up?"

"I don't think he believes me," she sighed and threw herself at the bed.

"He's a tough man to read, I'll give him that. But I don't think you meant to hurt her. Your powers are still so new you can't always control them. Though I will say I'm impressed you managed not to drench her."

Before McKenzie could respond, I caught raised voices in the hallway. "Mr. Bartow, I'm going to need you to come downstairs and answer a few more questions."

"Why? I told you everything I know," Trevor protested.

"Sir, your wife was poisoned."

13

———

Trevor stood in the hallway, mouth hanging open as he stared at Chief Hayes. I eased the door shut, trying to give the officers some semblance of privacy. After a mental count of ten, I heard footsteps echoing down the stairs. McKenzie still lay across the bed looking exhausted. I didn't blame her. So much had happened in such a short span of time. I was surprised my own body hadn't collapsed under the sheer weight of it all.

"I don't understand something," I said, eyeing the woman on the bed. "You saw that she was in trouble and you tried to help. That's admirable, but *why*?"

"No one else was going to do it," McKenzie answered.

"You don't know that. Someone might have noticed and done something if you hadn't."

"I don't think that's true. And I don't know, I'd kind of gotten used to seeing her. I never talked to her or anything, but she seemed so lonely, I wanted to help."

Her words caught me off guard. There hadn't been enough time while we were on the island for McKenzie to get a sense of Sheila's demeanor. "You saw her before two days ago?"

"Well, yeah. I've been there for about a month and I've seen her a couple times."

"And let me guess, she'd gone to see Paula at the Tea Shoppe."

"Yeah, like clockwork," McKenzie replied.

So, she had been going to the island for these purchases, not buying them online or some other way. That only raised more questions. How had Sheila found Paula? And why? What was so special about those teas that she'd not only make multiple trips a month to procure them, but keep them a secret from her family?

"Do you have any idea what she was doing there? Why make the trip out just to buy tea?'

McKenzie sat up and shrugged. "I never got close enough to hear their conversations. I just know she always looked so hopeful when she left and the next time she came, she looked so sad. Like whatever she'd been hoping for hadn't happened."

That seemed to fit with what I'd observed in my brief scroll through her Facebook feed. Still, I wanted to know why no one could find Paula. I pulled out my phone, beginning to pace the length of the bedroom. I could feel McKenzie watching me as I moved. I brought up a search on my browser and typed in 'The Tea Shoppe Haven Island' and waited for the results to populate.

There were only a couple of entries that appeared, one of which appeared to be the shop's official website. That would do just fine. I double tapped on the link and waited for it to open. The page was sparse, listing only the address on the island, a photo of a dark-haired woman with a caption reading *Paula, Owner*, and a phone number for inquiries. I suppose I could always call Paula and see if she answered. But that didn't answer the question of why Paula was in Sheila's orbit.

I nearly missed the note at the bottom of the page. It was in small font and I had to enlarge the page to read it properly: *Holistic healing herbal teas. To heal what ails you as nature intended.*

"She's a healer," I said, forgetting McKenzie was still listening.

"Who?"

"Paula. The tea shop lady. What if Sheila was ill, or thought she was, and sought out a less traditional method of curing whatever ailed her?"

It would explain why she was making such frequent trips and why they were so expensive. I bet if Paula was offering up those types of remedies, she could charge a premium, and people would pay it whether it was warranted or not. But could teas really help someone cure an illness? I made a mental note to check in with Maggie on that point.

Sorting out those questions could wait a minute. I needed to know whether Paula was even still around or if she'd fled the moment Sheila died. I returned to the website and tapped the shop's phone number. I waited for it to connect, turning my phone to speaker.

It rang three times before switching over to a recording. "You've reached Paula at the Tea Shoppe. I'm not in right now. Please leave a detailed message and I'll get back to you."

I ended the call before it could tell me to leave a

message. It was technically after business hours in most places, so it was reasonable she wouldn't answer her work phone. It could also suggest she'd abandoned her shop. I'd try again in the morning.

I needed to talk to Maggie about the teas; but not tonight. The events of the day suddenly crashed against me and I failed to stifle a yawn. I could see her in the morning or during my lunch break. She'd be able to tell me whether Paula and her teas were for real.

"We're going to figure out what happened to Sheila. If she was poisoned, it couldn't have happened too many places," I told McKenzie before stepping into the hallway.

"What if they can't figure it out?"

"The Chief and I may have our differences, but if there's one thing I know about him, he's a determined man. He won't stop looking until he unravels the truth."

In the back of my mind, I knew there was something else I should have asked her, some other piece of the puzzle to Sheila's demise. My brain was far too tired to focus on it long enough to remember what it was. I was never so happy to see my bed across the hall. I crawled beneath the covers and fell off to sleep in minutes.

My dreams swirled with a giant writhing storm of tea leaves that refused to obey me. They were brittle, sharp shards that a faceless woman controlled from just out of view. Every time I tried to exert control, they lashed out, leaving my hands and arms bloodied and raw. I reached with my magic, but there was nothing around me that could give me aid. The leaves were the only greenery, but they had fallen under this other witch's spell.

"You aren't going to stop them," an eerie voice called out amid the rattling of the brittle leaves.

A rush of heat slammed against my bruised and battered body, knocking me backward. I failed to steady myself and ended up toppling head over arse toward the hut where I'd found McKenzie. I braced, trying to cover my head with my arms to lessen the impact when everything around me went black.

I sat upright in bed, drenched in a cold sweat. I could feel the dampness seeping down my sides and shivered at the sensation. I groped for my phone to see the time. It was already five in the morning. A shower to clean up and clear my head was definitely in order as was an oversized cup of coffee.

By the time I'd let the warm water wash away the

stink and clammy feeling of the sweat, it was after six. Ginny's would be open now, even if the crowd populating it wasn't that numerous. The police presence from the night before had vanished at the B&B. That seemed strange if the police had determined Sheila had been poisoned. Wouldn't they want access to everyone who'd been with her the day of her death? Before leaving the B&B, I double checked Trevor's room. He lay sprawled on the bed, snoring. Either Chief Hayes trusted this man to not be a flight risk or he was confident enough Trevor wasn't a suspect anymore.

Making the trip down Main Street to Ginny's took no time at all and I was relieved to see the sign on the front door read 'Open' when I approached. I could see a couple of people inside. Ginny, in a rare instance, was not inside. I walked in to find Captain Merchant sitting at one end of the counter. A man I recognized, whose first name I recalled was Gerry, sat in a booth reading a newspaper. A spark of curiosity made me wonder if he'd ever caught up on the town's news. He'd been away for a while and had insisted on reading every issue of the paper from the library during that time. We'd first crossed paths when I'd been doing a deep dive into Vera and McKenzie's social media about a month ago. We'd seen each other a few times at Ginny's in the intervening time and without fail, he always sat with a newspaper in hand.

"Morning," I greeted and walked over to sit at the far seat at the counter. "How goes catching up on all of Brookhaven's latest news?"

Gerry looked up from his reading and smiled at me. "Good morning, dear. I'm all caught up, thanks for asking." He flashed the front page of today's paper as proof. "I haven't seen you in here this early in a while. Special occasion?"

"Just needed a bigger cup of coffee than I could get at home today," I answered through a yawn.

"Ginny's whipping up a pot in the back now."

I couldn't hide my surprise that Ginny Hayes was actually doing *work*. My eyes didn't deceive me as Ginny walked out with a carafe of coffee in one hand and a toasted bagel on a plate in the other. She set the bagel down in front of the Captain before approaching Gerry.

"Only you could make me break out the extra bold brew this early," she noted as she poured it into Gerry's mug.

"A man's got to be alert," he replied.

Ginny pivoted, looking at me with her lips pressed into a forced smile. "What can I get you?"

"Since you've already gone to the trouble to brew that, I'll take a large cup," I answered. "And eggs on toast. Wheat if you've got it."

"That will be a bit. The cook's not in yet."

"That's fine. I've got plenty of time."

Ginny retrieved one of the oversized cups from below the counter and filled it up before setting it in front of me. The scent hit me and any hint of sleep receded. I didn't know which blend Gerry had requested, but it would definitely do the job.

"I'm surprised you aren't in more of a frenzy with only a few months to go," Ginny said in a casual tone, addressing Gerry.

He looked up from the paper and chuckled. "Truth be told, if I'd had my way, he would have gone down to town hall and done it there. No need for a big showy affair."

I waited quietly, sipping the strong brew until Ginny relented and told me, "His son is getting married in November."

"Oh, cheers. That's grand."

Gerry waved off the remark. "Like I said, I'd have preferred something small, as it isn't his first trip to the altar. Not even his second," he continued with a snort. "But what can I say? I love my boy and he's asked to have a big wedding as his final hurrah. So, that's what he gets. Not that we have any idea where everyone is going to stay."

I held my tongue in offering up the B&B. That was Tania's purview, but I would mention it to her when I saw her next. She likely knew Gerry and could make the offer herself.

"Weddings and marriage are overrated," Captain Merchant said from the other end of the counter. "Just lead to drama and bitterness."

"That's not true for everyone," I replied.

"Trust me, it isn't worth the headache."

As he set his now-empty plate aside, I noticed a slender silver band on his left ring finger. Interesting that a man who was clearly married had such a dim view on the institution. Maybe he just didn't like spending money unnecessarily?

"You had to believe in it at some point," I replied, gesturing to his hand. "It couldn't have been all bad. I'm sure you were in love."

"Look, don't give marriage advice, lady. I don't see a ring on your finger."

"Oh, come on, how bad could the Missus be?" Ginny interjected, batting her lashes his direction. She leaned on the opposite side of the counter.

"She's leaving me for some punk yoga instructor or something. I should have seen it coming. My long hours working, gave her plenty of time to find a new *hobby*," he answered. The way his jaw hung slack after he'd spoken suggested he hadn't intended to make that confession. "And now she's trying to bleed me dry. Not that she needs the money working for all those rich folks out on the island."

Were the Captain and Corinne married? I didn't recall seeing a wedding band on her finger, but if his statement was true, she'd have abandoned that symbol.

"I'm sorry to hear that. If that's the case, then she didn't deserve you," Ginny replied.

Captain Merchant smirked at her compliment. "I'll take some of that coffee, too."

"Coming right up." Ginny paused, head cocked to one side, her hair cascading over one shoulder. "Sounds like our cook just got in. Your eggs and toast will be up, too."

I gave her a grateful nod and pulled out my phone. The jolt of caffeine had given my brain enough of a jumpstart to get me moving on unraveling why a tea shop owner would have wanted Sheila dead. I opened the message app on my phone and found Maggie's number.

'Can we meet for lunch? I've got some healing questions.'

I didn't expect a response right away, yet the three little dots populated almost immediately.

'Sure. Come by the clinic on your break.'

I sent her a thumb's up emoji just as Ginny appeared with my plate of food. I dug in, eager to start my shift at High Time so I could meet up with Maggie. Maybe she would have the answers I was looking for.

14

———

*L*unch couldn't come soon enough. There was a large part of me that just wanted to pick Maggie's brain about whether teas could be used to treat ailments properly. There was another, more insistent part, that just wanted to spend time with her. I'd not gotten up the courage to even admit that I fancied her. Besides, I had no confirmation she was even interested in me.

At noon on the dot, I clocked out and sprinted over to the clinic. Maggie stood outside, waiting for me. She looked up from her phone and her smile broadened into a grin.

"Hey," she greeted.

"Hi," I replied, resisting the urge to take her by the hand and lead her down to the boardwalk in search of food and a place to sit and talk. "Thanks for offering to help."

"Of course, although I'm sure I'd be more help if I knew what was going on. Your text was a little cryptic."

"I know, sorry about that. I'll explain everything."

I waited until after we'd bought sandwiches from a cart halfway down the boardwalk and found seats on a bench overlooking the water. I could still see Captain Merchant's ship moored in the distance.

"So, what's going on?" Maggie prodded.

I set my food in my lap. "So, the woman from the cruise was poisoned. I don't know what with, although the questions Chief Hayes asked made it sound like cyanide."

"Do I want to know how you found out something Rick Hayes knows that's related to a police investigation?" Maggie's brow arched.

"I may have borrowed Beau's camouflage to listen in on his questioning of Walter's sister," I admitted. "We found her by the way. Out on the island." I grinned in spite of myself. "Had a bit of a witch fight."

Maggie snorted. "Excuse me?"

"Well, when we got there, it seemed like McKenzie wasn't interested in talking to anyone, let alone her brother. So, I thought maybe it would be better to approach her, you know, witch to witch."

"Didn't go well, I take it?"

"Uh, well there were waves and trees, and yeah it was a bit of a mess. Thought I might drown a few times. But I got her to come back in the end. Just wish it hadn't meant me getting drenched three times over."

"I was at Ginny's last night when I heard rumblings about there being a person of interest in the death."

"Chief Hayes thought McKenzie did something since they found her fingerprints on the body. But she insists she was trying to flush whatever toxins were in her body out."

"A lot's happened since I saw you last," Maggie noted.

"And that's not all. There's this woman on the island, Paula, who runs a holistic healing tea shop and it looks like the dead woman, Sheila, might have been a long-term customer of hers. McKenzie told me she'd seen them together on the island a few times over the last few weeks. It's why she tried to help her when Sheila couldn't breathe."

"And you think the shop owner had something to do with poisoning her?" Maggie took a bite of her food, chewing it in contemplation. "That doesn't seem quite right for someone who is presumably paying her and giving her business."

"That's the bit I can't quite wrap my head around either. But maybe if I could understand what she was doing, or thought she was doing, it might help. I mean, if she's some sort of fraud and Sheila realized it ... if there was a confrontation, I could see Paula not wanting her to spread the word and damage her business."

"I'd need to get a better look at her set up, but long before the days of modern medicine, healers used herbs and plants to help treat all sorts of illnesses from common colds to counteracting poisons."

I'd been operating off the assumption that Sheila had been unaware she was being poisoned. What if she'd known and had gone to Paula in an effort to cleanse her body and it was too little, too late?

"So, you think Paula might have been trying to help her?"

Maggie shrugged. "I can't say one way or another. All I know is, if you're asking if it's possible to use plants and distill them into teas to help heal illnesses, then yes, it's possible. Is that what this woman was doing? I'd have to see it for myself."

"If you were going to try and counteract poison, what would you do?"

"Send them to a hospital."

"You've got magic," I said bluntly.

"And that magic has limits. For all the wonders we can perform, we aren't all-powerful. There are some things we aren't meant to meddle in."

"Humor me," I needled.

"I would need to know what sort of poison I was dealing with and I don't think there's anything specifically that could counteract cyanide. It's nasty stuff for a reason."

My expression faltered. It wasn't the answer I'd been expecting. "Right, yeah."

"Do you know what sort of teas she sells? That might give me some idea of what she's working with."

"I didn't see a list when I checked her website last night, but I can look again." I pulled up the browser tab and refreshed it. I didn't' expect to find different information on the page and for a moment it looked identical to the one I'd found last night.

"There, click that,' Maggie directed, pointing to a small icon at the very top of the page I hadn't noticed before.

I pressed my fingertip to the image on the screen

and a long list of names I didn't recognize appeared. My eyes glazed over as I scrolled.

"Send me that link and I'll look into it," Maggie said.

I copied it and sent it to her via text. "I just wish I could find Paula. Then we could just ask her what was going on, instead of sitting here speculating."

"As far as I know, no one in this town has the power to make people manifest out of thin air," Maggie said with a hint of amusement.

"I also have no idea how long she was being poisoned for. Was it just that day? Or had it been longer?"

"If it's cyanide, that doesn't take long to kill a person. I mean, when you see it in movies, it's pretty instantaneous."

"That's ingesting a lot all at once. What if whoever poisoned her gave her little bits over time?"

"It's possible that the cumulative effect would have killed her more slowly. But she would have noticed side effects I'm sure."

"What sort of side effects?"

"Fatigue? Diminished physical and mental function, maybe. I'm not an expert."

It was possible her change in behavior was the result of being poisoned over a long period of time.

Except that didn't seem to fit with the timing of the payments Sheila had made to Paula. It certainly seemed like she sought out Paula's services after the change occurred. That pointed back to Trevor.

He would have had the easiest access to his wife. But so far, he'd given no indication he'd wanted to harm her. He'd been surprised by her withdrawal from their relationship, rather than spiteful of it. Still, it might be worth another chat with the man.

"Have you tried to reach out to this healer?" Maggie's voice cut through the Trevor-shaped rabbit hole my brain currently had fell down.

"I called last night, but only got a message. I assumed she had gone home for the night. But she still hasn't given a statement to the police. That's worrying."

"You could try again since it's business hours."

Setting my food aside, I pulled up the shop's number in my phone's call history and hit redial. I set it on speaker and waited while it rang. The same message from last night came up after the fourth ring.

"It certainly seems like she's gone to ground," Maggie murmured.

"I know there's still got to be pieces to this I'm missing, but I can't see them," I sighed.

Maggie patted my arm. "Take a step back and think about what you do know."

"I know that Sheila had been making purchases from Paula for the last four months. I know that's around the time she started withdrawing from her friends and family. I know that according to the toxicology report, she had poison in her bloodstream," I recounted, suddenly recalling a piece of information I hadn't thought important at the time. "And Vinnie said she had an extremely elevated white blood cell count."

"That only happens when a person is sick," Maggie said.

"Would prolonged poisoning do that?"

"That sort of medicine is beyond my experience, but I could make a few calls and let you know."

"Thanks."

For now, it seemed that angle was a dead end. I could go back to Trevor and see if he remembered anything else. My phone beeped, reminding me I had a job to get back to.

"Call me or text me if you find anything medical that might explain things," I said and stood.

"What are you going to do?"

"After work, I'm going to see what else I can find out from Sheila's family. Her sister or her husband has to know something more that they aren't saying."

We parted ways and I headed back to High Time, trying to formulate my best approach to the conversations when I got back to Tania's after my shift. As I reached the employee entrance, the tiny hairs on the backs of my arms bristled. I looked around the parking lot, but I was alone. I closed my eyes and summoned the image of my magic, tapping into my power. I felt the grass, trees, and flowers around me.

'Show me what I can't see with my eyes.'

For the second time in as many days, the nature around me obeyed and let me see through its lens of greenery and new growth. In my mind's eye I moved across the street and found a female figure lurking in the shadows, toting a large case with three letters emblazoned on it in vivid gold: TSC.

Paula had come to Brookhaven after all.

The world came back to my normal senses in a disorienting whirl of color, sound, and sensations. I could hear the door to my right opening and a voice speaking, but it was distorted. My head spun and my stomach did an uneasy flop.

"Darcy, are you okay?" Sage's voice was in my ear now.

I turned and blinked my boss into focus. "Vertigo," I managed. It wasn't a lie. My entire equilibrium was off and I wasn't sure I could move under my own power.

My communion with the trees on Haven Island hadn't resulted in anything like this. Had Paula done something to me? Could she sense I'd spotted her from this distance? If she had, that meant she likely had magic of her own. It could explain how she'd stayed off the police radar so easily.

"Come on, why don't you come sit down?" Sage guided me into the break room and onto a bench. I hung my head between my knees as she retrieved water and a cool cloth. I draped it across my neck and let the dampness ground me.

"Did it just set in?" Sage's tone was soft, concerned.

I nodded mutely. I couldn't tell her I'd used magic and it had come back to bite me. Suggesting that I'd stood up too fast wouldn't hold water. There wasn't anywhere I could have stood up from. And if I told her it had been bad food, she'd probably think I had some sort of eating disorder.

"Given everything that's happened, if you need to take time ..." Sage began.

I shook my head. "No, it's passing. I'll be okay."

She eyed me, clearly not believing my words, but she eventually left me to sit alone in the break room. I needed to let someone know I'd seen Paula. I couldn't exactly explain it to the police, not unless I was ready to have an in-depth conversation with Chief Hayes. It would require an admission that I'd been looking into what had happened to Sheila, but I wasn't the only person who'd been snooping. In fact, he'd practically deputized his sister. Time for a little game of telephone.

I dialed Tania first. Her line rang three times before she answered. "Hello?" I could hear high-pitched voices in the background.

"Everything okay at home?"

There were garbled noises and then she said, "Mostly. Mr. Bartow has been pacing the living room in a nervous panic all morning. And Chief Hayes just came by to question the other family again."

That made sense. They'd been on the cruise with the Bartows. They might have seen something. "I don't suppose you heard anything about where she might have come into contact with the poison?"

"I'm afraid not."

"I'm not really surprised."

"You weren't calling just to check in on me, Darcy."

"Paula's in town."

"You act like I should know who that is," Tania replied.

"Right, sorry. She's the shop owner from the island. Well, one of them. The important thing is the police have been trying to find her to get a statement and she'd just vanished. But I saw her and she's in town."

"Did she come to the dispensary?"

"No ... I, uh, sort of used the surrounding plants to spy on her. I can't really explain it, but it was like they were amplifying my ability to see."

"Darcy, *felicidades*! Your powers are growing. Not that I'm surprised. Well, maybe a little at how quickly they're shifting."

"I'd love to explore all of that later, but right now we don't' have time. I need you to do me a favor and go over to Ginny's."

"Why am I paying Ginny a visit?"

"Because, I may have overheard Chief Hayes tell her to let him know if she heard anything useful. He's more likely to act on the information if it comes from her."

"And you can't deliver the message yourself, because ..."

"It's time sensitive and I can't leave work." Not if I still wanted a job and the ability to pay rent.

"I see. Where did you see her?"

"Up past Birch. But that was probably five minutes ago. She had a big case with her. I don't know what it was or why she's here, but just tell Ginny she's been spotted." I opened the website in my phone's browser again and screenshotted Paula's image. "I just texted you a picture to pass on to her, too."

"I will pass it along."

"And, if you wouldn't mind telling Sam to keep an eye out for her, that would be great. There's a piece of this whole thing I know I'm still missing, but I think Paula can point me where I need to look."

"Stay safe," Tania replied and ended the call.

There was little else I could do until my shift ended. So, I returned to the growth room. It could have been my imagination, but the usual whispers of the seedlings that ran like background noise in my head was eerily silent.

"It's just magic burnout," I told myself. My magic had failed me once before and it had taken Maggie's coaching and some meditation to get it back. I just had to give my body time to recover and recharge.

Being around the plants did help. The wooziness that had lingered dissipated and I felt almost back to normal by the time Sage stuck her head in. She ordered me to head home and get some rest.

"Do try to get some rest," Sage said as she accompanied me out the employee entrance.

"I will. Thanks," I replied before taking off at a light jog to the B&B.

I contemplated stopping by Ginny's, but doubted

the proprietor would divulge anything to me. I made it back to the B&B in time to see Simon's family climbing into a ride share car. Simon gave me a little wave before settling into a car seat. Tania stood on the front steps watching them.

"Rick deemed it okay for them to go home," Tania said simply.

"Did you get my message to Ginny?"

"I did. And Sam just came back. Our elusive tea shop owner appears to possess illusionary skills to rival our dear Beau."

I didn't like that she could disappear into thin air or more probably turn herself invisible. Why had she decided to show up, now? Those questions vanished from my mind as I heard Trevor Bartow's voice raised from within the B&B. Tania and I entered the foyer to hear the man arguing with someone who turned out to be Vinnie.

"I don't understand why you aren't listening?" Trevor shouted.

"Sir, I am listening, but you need to take a breath and explain what it is you think you found," Vinnie answered in a calm tone.

Trevor let out a frustrated breath. "I have been telling you for the last ten minutes that there's something off about my bank account." Trevor appeared from the kitchen, phone in hand.

I could make out some sort of banking app open on the screen. Trevor's anger bubbled over as Vinnie tried to reason with him and he threw the phone in my direction. Somehow, I managed to avoid the direct hit. Vinnie cast me an apologetic look as he man-handled the incensed man back into the kitchen. I bent to retrieve the phone to find it showed a series of withdrawal transactions that appeared to coincide with purchases from the Tea Shoppe. Withdrawals to the tune of $2,000 per transaction. That was certainly strange. From Sam's snooping I knew that Trevor had been trying to dispute the Tea Shoppe charges. But Sam hadn't mentioned anything about withdrawals. If Trevor had been telling me the truth and he didn't know anything about his wife's tea buying habits, it was too big of a leap to assume he'd simultaneously been taking out funds. No, the far more logical explanation pointed to Sheila making those withdrawals as well.

But why?

Not wanting to be seen as snooping, I turned the phone so its screen faced the floor and ventured into the kitchen long enough to set the item on the counter closest to Vinnie.

"You said you noticed large withdrawals," Vinnie said, trying to guide the conversation.

"Sheila handled the finances. If I opened that stupid app, it was maybe once every six months. Yesterday, I just got this feeling like I needed to log in. That's when I found all those weird charges and then I noticed all of these ATM withdrawals. They were from her card."

"And your wife didn't routinely withdraw large sums of money?" Vinnie already looked like he knew the answer.

"No, she didn't. I don't know why she was taking out so much and frequently."

I retreated back to the foyer. I leaned against the banister to find Beau lounging in mid-to-dark brown tones. Scratching his head, I told Tania, "It looks like Sheila was withdrawing large sums of money each month to coincide with her purchases from Paula."

"But they don't know what for?" she replied.

"No. And I can't figure out what Sheila would need it for, either."

'Be prepared.'

My brow knit together at Beau's statement. Usually his communications at least made sense, but this could have applied to any number of situations. I couldn't fathom what it had to do with finding Sheila's killer. Tania offered up a sympathetic look before gesturing to the stairs behind me.

"I'm going to turn over the room upstairs."

I watched her go, catching the sound of Walter's voice upstairs as she greeted him. He appeared at the top of the stairs and descended to the first floor faster than I thought possible.

"What's wrong?" I couldn't keep the whine from my tone.

"I can feel her," he said in a whisper.

"Who?"

"Paula."

"How? You've never met her."

"I'm not sure. Maybe because she was near McKenzie for so long, her aura rubbed off on her."

"Did Tania tell you she was in town?"

"I got this feeling a few hours ago and then she filled me on what you'd seen."

"So, where is she? Because a friend of mine went looking and couldn't find her."

His Adam's apple bobbed in his throat. "Here."

It took ages for the single word to register in my brain. "No, she isn't."

A sharp double knock on the front door sent me

leaping up off the landing and to the step above where Walter stood. He gave me a sidelong look before moving to open the door.

Much as she'd done when I'd used my magic to see her, she stood there with her large case.

"We need to talk," she said in a clipped tone.

Walter and I both stared at the woman standing on the front steps. She sported a deep complexion and dark brown hair, swept up into a knot on the top of her head. That sense of danger I'd felt when I realized she had come to town returned, accompanied by a confounding sense of safety.

"The police are going to want to talk to you," I said loudly.

"And I'll speak with them, but I need to talk to you first. Please, I think you'd want to hear what I have to say."

She wasn't wrong about that. I would wager everyone involved in Sheila's death would want to know the information this woman possessed. But I also knew that Vinnie was currently preoccupied with Trevor and his bizarre finances. That did raise the question of what happened to the temporary officer from last night and where was Chief Hayes?

"You aren't going to disappear on us are you?" I said, lowering my voice to a conversational pitch.

"No. Please, is there somewhere we can speak privately?"

If she was leaving the location of our chat up to me, then I had a destination in mind. "Come with me," I said before stepping around her and down the front steps.

She and Walter fell into step behind me as I led them down Main Street and to the clinic. I could see the lights still on in the front pharmacy area which boded well. Plus, Maggie had promised she'd look into how teas could be used to cure ills. To their credit, neither Paula nor Walter questioned why I brought them here.

The pneumatic doors whooshed open and Maggie popped up from behind the counter. She smiled when she spotted me, but her expression shifted to one of confusion as she spotted the people behind me.

"I hope you don't mind the unannounced visit, but Paula here has some information she thinks is important and seeing as she's a healer and you're a healer, I thought it best if we all had a chat together," I explained.

"So, she finally showed up," Maggie noted, eyeing the other woman with a look of distrust.

"Bold as brass, too, showing up on Tania's doorstep with police inside."

"Please, we don't have much time," Paula said, setting her case on the floor between her feet.

"Why didn't you talk to the police when all of this started?" I moved to stand opposite her. Walter took up a position behind her and Maggie remained behind the counter.

"I would say you wouldn't understand what I'm about to say, but I think we both know that isn't true," Paula began. "Like you said, I am a healer. I market myself as selling holistic remedies."

"I've been doing research. Most tea blends won't do more than soothe a sore throat or maybe drain your sinuses," Maggie quipped.

"Normally I would agree with you, but there is certain flora on the island that afford my wares an extra kick."

"You mean the poisonous plants they couldn't get rid of?" I retorted.

"You say poisonous, I say potent curatives under

the right circumstances."

"But Corinne Toomey told me that there were poisonous plants on the island," I pointed out.

Paula raised a brow. "You have communed with the flora on the island, did you feel any poison?"

"Well, no. But that doesn't mean it wasn't there."

"You're a charlatan," Maggie accused.

"My remedies work, but even I am not a miracle worker," Paula answered.

"Why was Sheila seeing you?" I pressed. "How'd she even find you?"

Paula kneaded her hands together in front of her. "I can't speak to how she found me, only that she did and if I could go back, I would decline her business."

"Why?"

"Because I realized very quickly I couldn't help her; not in the way she needed. I even tried to end the relationship, but she just offered me more money. I'm ashamed to admit I let greed win out."

"What sort of help did she need?" Maggie pressed.

"Modern medicine." The woman looked me right in the eye. "She came to me, because she'd been diagnosed with cancer."

Cancer?

I ran through the puzzle pieces I had in my head

—the withdrawing from her friends and family, the vague religious posts, the elevated white cell count in her toxicology. If she'd been too scared to tell her family about her diagnosis, it could have been why she'd kept her visits secret and why she'd sought Paula out in the first place. If she could find a miracle cure, she wouldn't have to ever admit the truth.

"Did she know that what you were giving her wasn't going to cure her?" My words came out hoarse.

"I think near the end she did. I thought I'd finally convinced her to at least tell her family what was going on. I don't get a lot of repeat customers on the island and I felt bad for her, so we talked. When I heard she'd come back with her family, I was hopeful she'd shared the news with them."

"I don't think they knew," Walter interjected.

"They definitely didn't know. Her sister and husband thought she was leaving him," I pointed out.

Paula's face fell. "I wish she'd gotten the chance to tell them the truth."

"She was in your shop right before she died. She told me she was waiting for an order. But you weren't anywhere to be found," I noted.

"I'd agreed to give her one last order of tea, but told her that my supply in the shop had run out. It takes time to cultivate and brew the right mixtures. By the time I came back there were police and I panicked."

"If you hadn't done anything illegal, why hide?" Maggie crossed her arms over her chest.

"Not all of what I harvest is strictly legal."

"What sort of tea did you give her? What was it supposed to do?" I interjected.

She bent and opened her case, revealing tiny rows of neatly labeled tea leaves. Somehow, I expected them to sing out to me like the greenery around me had begun to do. Only they were silent.

They're dead.

If Paula could commune with the leaves in this state, she was more necromancer than healer in my book. But a familiar sensation washed over me as she dug into a small pouch and pulled out recently picked leaves. They were still green and I could feel their promise to help. It had been the same feeling I'd gotten from the plants marked poisonous on the island.

"I saw this on the island."

"Wild rhubarb. Not something you want to mess with without the right know-how. And not the same sort you'd find in pies. Eating it will give you a wicked case of the runs. Distilling it into a tea slows the effects."

"You were hoping a diuretic was going to cure her cancer?" Maggie scoffed.

"Like I said, I did feel guilty giving her something I knew wasn't going to work, but she was desperate."

"The police know about her purchases over the last four months. But they also found large cash withdrawals during the same time," I offered, changing the direction of the conversation. "Why did you need the extra money?"

Paula shook her head. "She didn't give it to me. She set up a recurring payment with me for the tea and she insisted on picking it up, to avoid her husband finding out."

Picking it up in person. *Of course, how could I have missed it!*

"How did she get to the island? Corinne Toomey told me that only certain cruise companies have access to the island and they have to have manifests of who they are bringing. Privacy of the residents and all that."

"Captain Merchant," she said, as if it should have been the most obvious thing in the world.

"They knew each other?" Not that I'd seen them

interact much on the boat or even the island before her death, but it didn't seem likely that they had any kind of relationship. If she had been a long-time client of his, why wasn't he more broken up about her death?

"Did you ever see her pay him in cash?" I pressed.

"I only know he brought her, because he came ashore a couple of times to buy some supplies next door at Ollie's."

"Did they come with anyone else onboard?"

"Not that I saw. It's a small island, so it's hard to miss when a crowd comes through. No, most of the times when he brought her, she was alone."

"Could he have killed her?" I wondered aloud.

"Maybe, but what motive would he have?" Walter answered.

"All I know is, she came with him when she started buying from me. You'd have to ask him why he might want a well-paying client dead."

What had he said this morning at Ginny's? That his Corinne was leaving him and trying to bleed him dry? Money was always a powerful motivator. But that would give him a reason to want Corinne dead, not Sheila. There was still a piece missing.

"I think I might have an idea of what could motivate him to kill. We need to find him. Now."

"Shouldn't he be at Tania's?" Maggie replied.

I shook my head. "He has been sneaking off to Ginny's. I can't say for sure, but my gut tells me hasn't been staying at night either. At least I haven't seen him." I tugged my phone loose from my pocket and dialed Tania's number.

She answered on the first ring this time. "Please tell me you aren't off doing something reckless."

Not yet.

"Is Sam up for one more scouting trip?"

"Always," his voice crackled over the phone line.

"Head down to the boardwalk. I need you to check and see if Captain Merchant is on his boat. I'll meet you there."

I looked at the assembled group of people. It wasn't entirely who I'd choose to go running into danger with, but Maggie had proven she could have my back and Walter still had a vested interest in making sure his sister didn't end up prison. Paula, well she was the wild card, but it was a play I would have to risk.

"Come on. We're going to find the captain and put a stop to this before anyone else gets hurt."

17

———————

"This is the part where I tell you that you're being needlessly reckless," Maggie protested as she followed me along the darkened street toward the boardwalk.

"And that's why I've got you coming with me," I answered.

"We don't even know if he's there," Walter noted.

Sam materialized out of thin air at my elbow. "He's on board and he's acting super shady, girl."

I picked up the pace and approached the moored boat. I paused when I realized the gangplank was secured in the locked position onboard, complicating my plan to get onto the deck. As I tried to determine an alternate route, I glanced Paula's direction.

"You said he would sometimes come into Ollie's shop and buy supplies. Not to knock him, but he didn't exactly sell a lot I'd imagine that would suit a boat captain. I doubt he'd be sporting novelty shirts and hats."

"Ollie and I have a bit of a rivalry going. It's good-natured. But I remember him saying the man always bought him out of nuts."

Nuts. Oh, bloody hell.

"Please tell me they weren't almonds," I squeaked.

"Ollie's allergic to most other types so that's all he sells," Paula answered.

I caught Maggie's eye in the waning street-lights above us. She understood my concern. Cyanide came from almonds. There had been nuts on the pastries onboard two days ago and it appeared Sheila had eaten some of them. If she'd been using Captain Merchant for transportation for months and he'd been buying almonds, I sincerely doubted he just up and decided two days ago was the time to poison her. A little bit over a prolonged period of time would have slowly weakened her already compromised immune system. She likely would have attributed the symptoms to her cancer. For all I knew, it had fueled her desire to seek out Paula for more remedies.

"I still don't understand why he'd target her," Walter whispered.

"He told Ginny his wife was leaving him. They're going through a divorce and she's trying to take all his money."

"So, he kills someone? That makes no sense," he countered.

I didn't disagree. I couldn't fathom putting myself in the man's shoes to try and figure out his end goal, but I wouldn't have to. He was on the boat right now and it wasn't going anywhere if I could help it.

"You and Paula need to call the police and tell them what we've discovered," I addressed Walter.

"What are you going to do?" Anxiety tightened the skin around his eyes and mouth.

"See if we can get the Captain to open up about his misdeeds." I took Maggie's wrist. "I'm going to need back up."

She tugged her wrist loose long enough to slide her hand into mine and give it a reassuring squeeze. Now that we all had our marching orders, it was time to get on board that blasted boat. McKenzie's water powers would have been useful right about now, but she was back at the B&B and we didn't have time to wait for her to show up or even decide she wanted to help.

"I don't suppose we'd be tall enough to climb one over the other up the side?" I suggested.

Maggie shook her head. "No. But you have the ability to get us up there."

"How? I'm the plant girl, remember?"

Maggie grinned. "There are all sorts of plants in the water, you just have to know what you're looking for." She led me over to the edge of the boardwalk and dipped our entwined fingers into the cool water. I closed my eyes and reached out with the part of me that was my magic incarnate. It shot out of me like a laser, finding every bit of kelp and sea grass hiding beneath the surface.

I need to get up there.

Shoots of slick green and dark purple shot up from the water, twisting themselves into a lattice-work that draped up over the side of the boat. When it was finished, it was the equivalent of a rope net. I doubted its stability until Maggie pulled herself up with ease. Tania was right, I was going to have to sit down and really consider how my magic had grown in just the few weeks I'd been in town. I scrambled up the seaweed net and plopped onto the upper deck beside Maggie.

"Do you actually have a plan, besides confront potential murderer?" Maggie hissed in my ear.

"Confront potential murderer and get out alive?" I retorted as I inched along the darkened deck, clinging to the rail for guidance.

My ears perked up at the sounds coming from the navigation area. I hurried forward and used the element of surprise to go crashing into the small space. I found Captain Merchant ripping out pages from a paper ledger, crumpling them into a bin and flicking the ignition on a butane lighter.

"Stop!"

The man spun to face me, lighter still held aloft. His face was sweaty and there were dark, damp patches under his armpits. "You don't know how to keep your nose out of other people's business," he spat.

"I guess I'm like a bad penny, impossible to get rid of. How about you step away from that ledger though and we can talk. I don't really think burning evidence is going to sit well when the police arrive," I said.

"I'm on a boat you idiot," he scoffed, as if that meant he was untouchable.

"I think we both know you've come to the end of the line. The police are on their way. This town isn't very big, so it's not going to take them more than five minutes to get here and board your boat. Now, I don't know the Chief well, but I am certain he'd frown on destroying evidence."

"They can't prove anything," he said, starting to pace in the cramped cabin. He dropped the lighter and it ignited the contents of the bin. I'd seen him looking at a ledger on his phone the other day. Had that been different than these records? Or did he have a separate ledger for the solo trips he'd made with Sheila?

"Can you at least tell me why you did it?"

"She wants everything. But half of zero is still zero," he said with a cackle.

"Who wants everything?" Maggie stepped up beside me.

"My wife," he spat.

"How does killing Sheila put a stop to her getting any of your money?"

"Death is bad for business. Could get me shut down for who knows how long. Maybe even shuttered completely."

"So, you killed her to shut down your business? Why not just close it down if that's what you wanted?" I replied.

"Because if I just closed it down, she'd still get money."

I caught Maggie shaking her head out of the corner of my eye. "Even if you went bankrupt, your creditors could still come after you. You murdered a woman in cold blood for nothing."

The Captain shook his head. "She was dying anyway. It was a mercy really. And she would have kept paying me until she died. She wouldn't take no for an answer. Just threw more money at me."

I thought I heard the sounds of sirens in the distance and prayed they weren't an illusion. "How'd you do it?"

"You'd be surprised what you can find on the internet. Even simple ways to distill cyanide."

"Buying out Ollie's stock of almonds," I confirmed.

"She liked those stupid pastries, so I always made sure to have them on hand whenever she came. Just a little here and there. I upped the doses each time. I didn't think she'd make it this long."

Paula's tea might not have been a cure for cancer, but if it had caused her to have the runs then maybe her body purged enough of the toxin to keep her alive longer. It was then that I noticed the container of murky liquid in his hands. He'd distilled it. Where the rhubarb hadn't felt poisonous in my presence, his concoction turned my stomach even before he unscrewed the lid.

Maggie moved like a blur, trying to wrestle the container from his hands before I could stop her. Everything moved in slow motion as the contents sloshed onto her face and into her mouth and nose. I was vaguely aware of a shriek echoing in the tight quarters that I realized too late was my own.

Maggie fell to the floor, limp and motionless. Captain Merchant staggered back, eyes wide. His head whipped between Maggie's prone form and me, as if trying to decide if this would now be enough to get him what he wanted.

Like Hell.

The anger that had erupted within me on the island returned with a vengeance. I could feel roots deep within the ocean beneath me responding to my siren call to protect Maggie. The makeshift rope net materialized first, unfurling itself and undulating in midair. The captain let out a garbled noise as the kelp twisted around him, cocooning him in place. Other, thicker shoots erupted through the bottom of the boat to anchor him in place.

The siren wails were louder now. They were

coming. I collapsed at Maggie's side as she rasped for air.

Please, Chief, hurry.

THE TIME IT TOOK FOR VOICES TO SHOUT FROM beyond the boat felt interminable. I couldn't make out their words as I cradled Maggie to me. I knew I needed to do something or she was going to die. Poison like this was fast acting and I couldn't seem to rouse myself to combat it.

'*Purge.*'

Beau sat on top of the ship's wheel opposite me. He blinked slowly in his reptilian way, waiting for me to catch on to his meaning. It hit a moment later and a plan sprung fully formed in my head. I just hoped it would work as I intended.

I held out one hand and felt for the tingle I'd sensed from the freshly cut rhubarb in Paula's case. I let my power connect to it through nature and pictured myself summoning it from the case on the boardwalk. My hands twitched and then the tips of my fingers burned from the contact and I let out a soft sound of surprise that it had actually worked. A moment later, the burning retook my focus. I could understand now why the developers had thought this plant was poisonous at first. It left angry red marks on my skin as I wrenched Maggie's mouth open and shoved the leaves in. I worked her jaw to chew the contents and did my best to massage her throat to trigger her swallow reflex.

Now all I could do was wait. The very thing Paula had peddled to Sheila for her cancer might be the thing that could actually save Maggie's life. I heard loud metallic groaning and a concussive thud. I assumed Chief Hayes had found a way aboard via the gangplank. Even as I heard footfalls on the deck outside, it still felt like they were moving too slow.

Time stood still as I waited for the rhubarb to take effect. I prayed I hadn't been too slow to act. Hot tears stung my eyes, blurring my vision as Maggie's body began to stir and twitch. I squeezed my eyes shut to keep the tears at bay and focused all of my attention on the woman in my lap. I rolled her onto her side and began thumping on her back, hoping it would rouse her enough to vomit up the poison.

I shouldn't have wished so hard, because the retching sounds echoed in my ears as Chief Hayes appeared in the doorway, weapon drawn. He stowed it upon seeing the Captain's floral binds.

"What happened?" his voice was soft as he knelt beside me.

"He had poison. She tried to get it from him, but he hit her with it."

Maggie gave a soft moan and tried to sit up before collapsing back to the floor. Her entire body was covered in the sickly stench of flop sweat. It matted her short hair to her head even more and all I wanted to do was hold her and tell her she was going to be okay.

"He was trying to get his business shut down so he wouldn't have to pay his wife money in their divorce," I explained as the Chief produced a switch blade and began cutting away the dense plants bound around the Captain's arms and wrists. Just enough space to secure handcuffs.

"Mr. Lawson filled me in." he hauled the Captain to his feet and shoved him out of the space and into Vinnie's waiting arms. "You know, you put yourself in harm's way tonight for no reason."

"I had a perfectly good reason. A woman was dead and I needed to know why. I promised a friend I'd help find his sister and she was tied up in this case too."

"I admire your sense of loyalty Miss Ingram. To your friends and to people you barely know. I may not like the fact you keep stepping into my investigations, but my gut tells me you're not so bad to have around." He hooked a thumb over his shoulder. "I do like getting my suspects gift-wrapped."

A paramedic appeared in the doorway, ready to try and treat Maggie. Between Chief Hayes and I, we managed to get her upright enough to escort her out of the cabin and onto a waiting stretcher. She clutched my hand tight, her eyes barely slits.

"Thank you," she managed.

Those two words were enough to tell me that she was going to be okay. I held her hand all the way down the gangplank and back onto solid ground. I forced myself to release my grip on her hand as they loaded her into an ambulance.

"You aren't going to charge McKenzie are you?" I addressed the Chief. "She was just trying to help and it went wrong."

"Charging her doesn't serve justice," he replied.

A weight lifted from my shoulders. At least I could keep my word to Walter that McKenzie would be okay. I didn't know what would happen to them next, but at least they wouldn't be separated by plexiglass. As I rejoined Walter on the boardwalk, I felt Beau's tiny claws on my shoulder and I relished his familiar weight. There was still so much I didn't know about how his magic worked and he, like Sam, was tight-lipped on the specifics. Regardless, I was grateful he appeared when he did. Also I was beginning to believe, if not him, then perhaps some other larger force had brought Paula to us right when I needed her most, too.

"Did you know I was going to need those leaves?" I asked as we started toward the police station. In time, we'd all have to give statements about tonight's events.

"I can't see the future if that's what you're asking. But I did get a feeling that I needed to be here. Maybe it's because we both commune with plants and nature? I just knew I needed to pick some fresh rhubarb before I came."

"If you hadn't, my friend would be dead right now. I don't like your methods, but I owe you."

She gave me an understanding nod before separating from the pack to speak with Vinnie. The doors slid open behind me and I spun to find Tania walking in. I didn't bother asking how she knew where I'd be. Sam or Beau could have alerted her and I doubted the showdown on the boat would go unnoticed for long in this town.

Tania didn't speak. She simply wrapped me in a tight embrace. Sometimes having an empath for a friend was brilliant. We stood there for a long while until I felt like all of the tension and worry had drained out of me, leaving me exhausted and raw. Sleep would heal what ailed me now. With some rest and time, I trusted Maggie would heal, too.

"Let's go home," Tania whispered.

18

―――――――

I had never been more grateful to find an open table at Ginny's or to see its namesake sitting in her place of honor at the center of the counter. I needed that sense of normalcy after the last week. She wrapped her fingers around an oversized mug of coffee, ready to hold court. Ginny turned in my direction and our gazes met. I tensed as she slid off her stool and approached my table.

"You aren't so bad to have around," she proclaimed.

"Uh, thanks?" I replied.

Without seeking permission, she sat down across from me. "Rick won't ever say it, but he's grateful you helped him catch Captain Merchant."

She was right, those were words I never believed

Chief Hayes would ever say to or about me, or Ginny for that matter. "Yeah, well, sticking my nose in put my friends in danger. And I didn't want that to happen."

Ginny waved a hand, dismissing my discomfort. "We're more resilient around here than you think."

I took note of the royal *we* as she spoke. It was no secret she saw herself as the unofficial head of Brookhaven, controlling its rumor mill as it were. Though I couldn't be annoyed at her, because she clearly cared for the wellbeing of the people in this town, including Maggie.

"I'm just sorry a woman had to die to uncover what was going on out on the island," I said.

"For what it's worth, I was wrong," Ginny said, barely getting out the last word.

"Wrong about what?" I was enjoying her squirm under the weight of her own admission. Did her ability to pull the truth out of people apply to herself, too?

"When you first came here, I thought you were just going to agitate things, unbalance our carefully curated ecosystem. And yes, you definitely did shift things, but it's been for the better. Magic goes stagnant if it's left unexplored and we've been more than a little lax about using it for bigger things lately. So, thank you for pushing us ... for pushing me."

That was the first time anyone outside of the B&B or Maggie had spoken about magic as a real, tangible thing. "I appreciate you saying that." I offered my hand across the table. "And just so you know, I respect your powers. I hope one day I have as much control as you."

She took my hand, gave a single firm shake, and slid out of the booth. "Something tells me you will, with enough time and practice."

She gave me a small smile and nod. Whatever tension had existed between us, was for the time being resolved. We weren't friends by any definition of the word, but we could count each other as acquaintances. Also I truly did hope that Ginny and I could co-exist and learn from each other one day.

The bell above the door sounded and Walter walked in followed by McKenzie. She still looked shell-shocked to be in the company of people she could trust. She'd been overly apologetic about not being there to help confront the Captain and for not divulging the information sooner about him being Sheila's transport to and from the island. Walter and I had both assured her that she would have only been in more danger if she'd been present and that she couldn't be expected to recall every detail all at once. I was halfway out of the booth to greet them when Walter gestured for me to sit back down.

"Hi," I said once they'd settled across the table from me. "How are you holding up?"

"Better now that the police don't think I killed someone with magic." McKenzie whispered the last word like she still didn't believe it was okay to say it aloud. "The Chief officially told me that they aren't going to charge me with anything, because it wasn't the primary cause of her death."

"The night of the Captain's arrest, he told me that arresting you wouldn't serve justice. He puts a lot of stock in what is right and what is just. And for whatever reason I think he understands you were new to your power."

""I still can't believe there are other people out there like me."

"This town is downright full of them," I noted. "It's something that took some getting used to for me, too. But I had people to help me acclimate; like Tania and Maggie." My chest tightened for a split second at the mention of her name.

"I'm glad your friend is going to be okay," McKenzie added.

I didn't like my friends nearly dying on me. I

took it rather personally, but Maggie had insisted she would be fine and I didn't need to nurse her back to health. Leave it to a healer to be a poor patient. Still, I'd convinced her to keep Beau in her apartment just to be on the safe side. If nothing else, he could reach Sam who could find Tania or I quickly enough.

"Thank you for believing that I didn't hurt that woman."

I glanced to Walter. "You should be thanking your brother. He never gave up on you. Besides, there was not a reason we could think of where you'd want to harm a total stranger. From everything Walter told me about you, it wasn't who you are."

"I told you I had your back, Kenz," Walter said, nudging her shoulder with his.

"If I'd just been able to control my powers, maybe I could have saved her life," McKenzie sighed.

"Well, now you've got time to figure out how to hone your skills. Believe me, I've been there and I'm still there most days," I offered.

She smiled at me, but it didn't reach her eyes. She'd been on her own for months, hiding out on that island for weeks, and nearly been accused of murder. I didn't blame her for being eager to get out of town.

I looked to Walter. "Where are you going now?"

"I think we're going to head home and see what we can figure out together."

"I'm not afraid of this power anymore. But between you and me, I'm not looking forward to having my big brother constantly tell me what I'm feeling."

"I told you, Kenz, I'm not an empath. I can just sense people. It's completely different," Walter replied.

"Whatever," she muttered with a half-smile. I didn't need to be able to read emotions to know she was really glad he was going to be there for her.

"I'm glad you're finding the place where you feel safe to practice your craft. At least you didn't have to cross an ocean to find it," I said, my chest tightening. Thinking of London still brought with it waves of sadness for what I'd left behind. Beneath all of that melancholy, though, lingered a tiny nugget of hope that perhaps one day I'd be able to set things right with my parents and we could be in each other's lives again. But that day was a long time coming, if ever.

"No, I just ran across the country instead, and I

couldn't even do that right," McKenzie sighed, interrupting my thoughts.

Is she talking about her run-in with Vera?

Until now, there hadn't been a good time to broach the subject. Only now seemed a good time and place to try, especially if she was opening herself up to questions. I inhaled and launched in.

"I don't know how much you were aware of what happened in town while you were out on the island, but Walter and I actually crossed paths before."

McKenzie's brow wrinkled. "Why?"

"Because a young woman was killed. She had your phone and wallet on her. We thought for a bit there that you'd been killed," I explained.

Color warmed McKenzie's cheeks. "I didn't know that."

"But you did know her," Walter prodded.

"No. I mean, we met on a bus out of New York. I'd ended up there maybe a month or two ago." She twisted a few strands of dark hair around her index finger. "I wouldn't recommend trying to hide out there."

I could only imagine the safety risks she'd faced. I didn't blame her for wanting to get out. "What made you come out this way?"

"I don't know. I just picked a bus going east and it

happened to come this way. We stopped in Springfield and I got off to use the restroom at the bus depot." She glanced at her brother. "I hate the bathrooms on buses and planes. Anyway, this other girl who'd been on the bus was in the next stall and when she came out, I could tell she'd been crying."

"Vera?" I prodded.

"That's what she said her name was. She said she'd just broken up with her boyfriend and she was worried he would come looking for her."

She had told this stranger the truth.

I wanted to ask why Vera would have entrusted McKenzie with such sensitive information, but realized it was a calculated move. Vera had probably seen the striking resemblance between them and pegged McKenzie as a mark. She might have been running from her drug dealer ex-boyfriend, but she'd no doubt picked up a few unsavory skills along the way.

"We sort of bonded over our shared worry about being found," McKenzie continued. "We got to talking and ended up sitting next to each other the rest of the way."

"How'd she end up with your stuff?" Walter interjected.

"I guess I hadn't been paying very close attention. Maybe she saw me put my wallet and phone back in my pocket. By the time I realized she'd taken them, she and the bus were long gone."

If only she'd known Vera and her belongings hadn't been nearly as far away as she'd envisioned. "You could have reported the theft to the police," I noted.

She shook her head. "I know it sounds stupid, but I had it in my head that if I did that, somehow Walter would find me and I just wasn't ready for that. Plus, I didn't have an ID anymore. How was I going to prove who I was?"

They could have run her fingerprints. That might have actually ruled her out as the potential victim in Vera's death sooner. In fact, it could have cleared up that confusion altogether.

"How did she die?" McKenzie's voice came out soft.

"That ex-boyfriend she was running from caught up to her and strangled her," I answered. The memory of finding Vera's body crammed into the trunk of Tania's VW bug came to mind and I shuddered.

"I'm sorry. Theft aside, she seemed nice."

"Truth be told, I don't think any of us really knew her. But she didn't deserve to die," I said.

We fell into silence as the ambiance of the space settled around us. It was comforting and surprising how quickly this place had come to feel like home. It might not be the right place for McKenzie and Walter's next chapter, but it suited me just fine.

"What are you going to do now?" McKenzie's voice interrupted my thoughts.

"Oh, go back to tending my plants and learning how to control my magic. And keep my head down. I'm glad we could sort things out for you two, but I don't know that the sleuthing business is for me."

Both Walter and McKenzie smiled back at me in understanding. As we sat there, one of the waiters came over with three cups of coffee we hadn't ordered. There was a folded over napkin stuck under my cup and I caught Ginny's eye when I looked up. She winked.

I unfolded the napkin to find a single line of neat penmanship, with a phrase that had clearly been written after I'd spoken.

Never say never.

QUICK AUTHOR'S NOTE

WHEN I STARTED THIS SERIES, I KNEW I WAS SETTING myself up to have two related cases in the first two books. From the moment I invented McKenzie and Vera, there really wasn't any other option than to have one be the victim and the other still be missing at the end of book 1. And so, came the idea for the second book. The interesting thing about many books in this series, is I came up with titles (and bought covers) for them long before I started writing. So in a way, I had no choice but to find some sort of water theme for this book.

And that's where McKenzie's powers came from and I'd initially had an idea that there would be more victims, but as I worked on the first draft of the story, I realized that I was struggling to come up with reasons why the killer would target multiple people (or why anyone would keep going on a cruise where people kept dying). So, I stuck with just the one victim that McKenzie tried to save.

I hadn't anticipated the growth in Darcy's powers either, but I have to admit I kind of like the expansion she experienced. Don't piss her off unless you want to be snared in vines. Don't worry, though, that won't always be her trick. Although as signature moves go, it's pretty handy. I enjoyed having her feel more established in the ecosystem of Brookhaven, while also setting up the next story. It wasn't as outright a set up as this book, but I'm pretty sure if you read carefully, you can guess where Darcy's next mystery takes her.

TURN THE PAGE FOR A GLIMPSE AT HIGH FIDELITY....

<u>HIGH FIDELITY</u>

Love's a witch!

Darcy finally feels like she's found her place in small town Brookhaven. Her magic is blossoming and she's even worked up the courage to ask the town healer to be her date to the biggest wedding in town.

But Darcy's romantic happiness takes a backseat when the groom turns up dead. Darcy knows she shouldn't get involved in yet another murder investigation, but when her date winds up as a suspect, she'll do anything to set the record straight.

The more Darcy follows the evidence--both magical and mundane--the more she unravels about the groom's With a string of ex-wives, there's no shortage of suspects. But, as Darcy inches closer to the real killer, her own life winds up in danger. A final confrontation is inevitable. But is Darcy's magic enough to save her this time and bring a murderer to justice?

Scan the QR code to buy High Fidelity today

ABOUT THE AUTHOR

S.E. Biglow is the pen name of *USA Today* bestselling author Sarah Biglow. She lives in Massachusetts with her husband and son. She is a licensed attorney and spends her days combatting employment discrimination as an Investigator with the Massachusetts Commission Against Discrimination.

You can find an up-to-date list of all my books here